HIGH PLAINS FURY

The man slashed at Fargo's throat and he jerked back and slammed his boot against the man's knee. The small man stayed on his feet. Dropping into a crouch, he snarled with an accent, "Bastard. We will stop you before you can begin."

Fargo had no time to wonder what he meant. The man came at him slashing and thrusting. Fargo dodged, twisted, sidestepped. Then a quick flick of the other's blade cut his left sleeve and the biceps underneath. The cut wasn't deep but it drew blood.

Fargo boiled with fury. Springing out of reach, he tucked at the knees and slid his hand into his right boot, molding his palm to the hilt of his Arkansas toothpick. As the small man lunged, he streaked the toothpick to meet the other's blade. Steel rang on steel.

Now it was the small man who sprang back. "This is taking too long, big man," he growled with that accent of his. "The soldiers could come." And just like that, he whirled to run off.

Fargo wasn't about to let him. He leaped to put himself between the man and the tent opening but forgot about the chair he had kicked. He was reminded when his legs became entangled and he crashed to the ground.

The last glimpse he had of his would-be killer was of the man's wiry frame dashing out the flap.

THE
TRAILSMAN
#383

HIGH PLAINS
MASSACRE

by
Jon Sharpe

A SIGNET BOOK

SIGNET
Published by the Penguin Group
Penguin Group (USA) Inc., 375 Hudson Street,
New York, New York 10014, USA

USA | Canada | UK | Ireland | Australia | New Zealand | India | South Africa | China

Penguin Books Ltd., Registered Offices: 80 Strand, London WC2R 0RL, England
For more information about the Penguin Group visit penguin.com.

First published by Signet, an imprint of New American Library,
a division of Penguin Group (USA) Inc.

First Printing, September 2013

The first chapter of this book previously appeared in *Terror Trackdown*, the three
hundred eighty-second volume in this series.

 REGISTERED TRADEMARK—MARCA REGISTRADA

ISBN 978-0-451-41950-7

Printed in the United States of America
10 9 8 7 6 5 4 3 2 1

The Trailsman

Beginnings . . . they bend the tree and they mark the man. Skye Fargo was born when he was eighteen. Terror was his midwife, vengeance his first cry. Killing spawned Skye Fargo, ruthless, cold-blooded murder. Out of the acrid smoke of gunpowder still hanging in the air, he rose, cried out a promise never forgotten.

The Trailsman they began to call him all across the West: searcher, scout, hunter, the man who could see where others only looked, his skills for hire but not his soul, the man who lived each day to the fullest, yet trailed each tomorrow. Skye Fargo, the Trailsman, the seeker who could take the wildness of a land and the wanting of a woman and make them his own.

*1861, the Black Hills—where the
rumor of gold results in a river of blood.*

1

Skye Fargo wasn't expecting anyone to try to kill him.

Fargo had sat in on a poker game at Paddy's, a tent saloon within shouting distance of Fort Laramie. The Irishman who ran it believed that one day soon a town would spring up and he would build a real saloon and make money hand over fist.

Fargo liked Paddy Welch. Paddy was one of the few men breathing who could down as much liquor as he could and not keel over from whiskey poisoning.

Fargo had just been dealt two queens and two tens and asked for a card and been given another queen. Lady Luck was riding on his shoulder. Now all he had to do was play it smart and build up the pot.

Then two things happened.

The first was a hand that tapped Fargo on the shoulder as someone cleared his throat. "Excuse me. Are you Skye Fargo, the scout?"

About to refill his glass, Fargo turned his head.

A young lieutenant in a clean uniform stood ramrod straight as if on parade, awaiting his answer.

"No," Fargo said.

"You answer the description I was given by Colonel Jennings. He said to look for a big man in buckskins, with a beard and blue eyes."

"Jennings, you say? Never met the man." Fargo filled his glass and set the bottle down.

"How peculiar." The lieutenant shifted his weight from one polished boot to the other and gnawed on his bottom lip. He had no chin to speak of and a pale complexion, and for a soldier, looked about as intimidating as a kitten. "Do you know this Fargo, then? Could you point him out to me?"

"Never met the man."

The other players were staring. One, in particular, had his mouth wide in surprise. As well he should, since Bear River Tom had been a friend of Fargo's for years. "Well, tits," he said, and laughed.

The lieutenant blinked. "Did you just call me tits, mister?"

"He calls everything tits," Fargo said. "They're all he ever thinks about. If he could, he'd eat them for breakfast."

"Would I ever," Bear River Tom agreed, with a vigorous bob of his chin. "Smeared with honey. Or maybe peaches and cream."

The lieutenant wasn't amused. "I don't know how tits got into this. I'm here on official business. And who might you be, anyhow? You wear buckskins. You're not Fargo, are you?"

"Do I have blue eyes?" Bear River Tom said, and opened his brown eyes as wide as they would open. "Am I so handsome that ladies rip their clothes off and throw themselves at my feet?"

"No," the lieutenant said. "Don't take this personal, but you're sort of ugly."

Fargo had just tilted his glass to his lips and burst out laughing and coughing.

"Tits and cream," Bear River Tom said, and introduced himself. "Who are you, green boy? And why are you interrupting our game?"

The youngster gave a slight bow. "Lieutenant Archibald Wright, at your service. I'm not that green, I'll have you know. I've been on the frontier two months now."

"Two whole months," Bear River Tom said.

"Colonel Jennings would very much like to talk to this Fargo character," Lieutenant Wright said, "and he tasked me with finding him."

"Don't you hate being tasked?" Bear River Tom said.

"Have you any idea where I can find him?"

"He was planning to light a shuck for Denver," Fargo said.

Wright cocked his head. "I thought you just said you've never met the man."

"I heard it from the barkeep."

"Oh. Colonel Jennings will be terribly disappointed. The matter is most urgent."

Fargo's curiosity was piqued and he asked, "What is it about, anyhow?"

"You won't believe me if I told you," Lieutenant Wright said. "It sounds preposterous."

"Tell me anyway."

"I'm afraid the information is confidential."

"You can trust us, boy," Bear River Tom said. "I can keep my mouth shut except around tits."

"Must you mention them with every breath?" Lieutenant Wright shook his head. "I'd better keep searching in case this Fargo hasn't left yet. The colonel was most insistent." He gave another sort of bow and marched stiffly off.

"What that boy needs," Bear River Tom said, "is a night with a handful of tits. It'd take a lot of that starch out of him."

"Can we go five minutes without hearing about tits?" Fargo said.

Bear River Tom grinned and opened his mouth to say something. Suddenly his eyes grew wide again.

Fargo glanced over his shoulder, thinking that the young lieutenant was coming back. Instead, a much smaller man was coming at him with a knife poised to thrust.

2

"Look out, hoss!" Bear River Tom bellowed.

Fargo was already in motion. He heaved upright and twisted even as the man with the knife lunged. The blade missed his chest by a hair.

He was still holding his glass and he dashed the whiskey in the would-be killer's face. The man backpedaled, wiping at his eyes with a sleeve.

Letting go of the glass, Fargo kicked his chair at the man's legs. It caught him across the shins, eliciting a howl of pain and anger.

Fargo was sure he'd never seen the man before. He wouldn't forget someone who had an eye patch over his left eye and bore a large scar on his right cheek. The man's clothes consisted of common woolens and boots and a small cap.

Fargo pegged him as a river rat, but what was a river rat doing so far from a river? That was a minor puzzle compared to the important question: Why in hell was the man trying to kill him?

Fargo wanted him alive, which was why he didn't resort to his Colt. Taking a quick bound, he gripped the man's wrist and drove his other fist into the man's scarred cheek. For most that would be enough to bring them down. Fargo wasn't puny. But all the small man did was give his head a shake, hiss like a struck snake, and wrench his arm free.

The other players, momentarily riveted in astonishment, now scrambled to get elsewhere.

Except for Bear River Tom, who whooped, "Give him hell, Skye!"

Fargo ignored his friend and focused on staying alive.

The man slashed at his throat and he jerked back and slammed his boot against the man's knee.

The small man stayed on his feet. Dropping into a crouch, he snarled with an accent, "Bastard. We will stop you before you can begin."

Fargo had no time to wonder what he meant. The man came at him slashing and thrusting. Fargo dodged, twisted, sidestepped. Then a quick flick of the other's blade cut his left sleeve and the biceps underneath. The cut wasn't deep but it drew blood.

Fargo boiled with fury. Springing out of reach, he tucked at the knees and slid his hand into his right boot, molding his palm to the hilt of his Arkansas toothpick. As the small man lunged, he streaked the toothpick to meet the other's blade. Steel rang on steel.

Now it was the small man who sprang back. "This is taking too long, big man," he growled with that accent of his. "The soldiers could come." And just like that, he whirled to run off.

Fargo wasn't about to let him. He leaped to put himself between the man and the tent opening but forgot about the chair he had kicked. He was reminded when his legs became entangled and he crashed to the ground.

The last glimpse he had of his would-be killer was of the man's wiry frame dashing out the flap.

"Son of a bitch." Fargo kicked the chair, heaved to his feet, and gave chase. He burst into daylight and glanced both ways.

The collection of cabins and tents that some folks claimed would one day become a town covered about seven acres. Many were so close together, they practically touched. The man with the eye patch could have darted into any one of half a dozen gaps.

Fargo ran to the nearest but there was no sign of his attacker.

"Did you lose him, pard?"

Bear River Tom and some others were emerging from the tent saloon.

"I reckon so," Fargo said in disgust.

"Who was he? Why was he trying to stick you?"

"Beats the hell out of me." Bending, Fargo slid the toothpick into its ankle sheath, making sure it was snug.

"Maybe he has a hate for handsome devils," Bear River Tom joked. "Him with that patch and that scar."

"You're not funny." Fargo examined the cut in his arm. It would heal readily enough but it stung like the dickens.

"He almost had you."

"Don't remind me."

It was then that someone cleared his throat and the voice of young Lieutenant Wright said from behind them, "Perhaps you can explain to me why Bear River Tom called you 'Skye'?"

Fargo turned. "You must not have heard right."

"I heard him as clear as anything," Wright said testily. "Play me for a fool once, shame on you. Play me for a fool twice, shame on me."

"Gosh," Bear River Tom said, "you're a poet."

"Stay out of this, you lump," Lieutenant Wright said, and jabbed a finger at Fargo. "You lied to me, sir. You *are* Skye Fargo, are you not?"

"I cannot tell a lie," Fargo said.

"I'm not amused by your antics. I assume you pretended not to be you so I wouldn't interfere with your poker game."

"That's good assuming," Bear River Tom said. "And why am I a lump?"

Lieutenant Wright ignored him. "As I've already explained, Mr. Fargo, Colonel Jennings sent me to find you. His exact words were that I'm to bring you to him whether you want to come or not."

"Hold on a minute," Fargo said. "At least let me finish the hand I was playing before that son of a bitch jumped me." He was thinking of his full house.

"Uh, pard," Bear River Tom said. "When you dropped your cards they landed face up on the table. We all saw what you had." He grinned. "I'm folding."

"Me too," another player said.

A third nodded.

"Serves you right for lying to me," Lieutenant Wright said. "Liars never prosper, or haven't you heard?"

"Isn't he adorable?" Bear River Tom said.

"Well, hell," Fargo said.

3

Lieutenant Wright knocked, and when they were bid to enter, Wright opened the door and stood aside for Fargo and Bear River Tom.

Colonel Jennings had gray at the temples and the air of a man who had seen it all. He was military through and through, a career man who never let regulations get in the way of doing what was right. "So you found him."

"Yes, sir," Lieutenant Wright said, and launched into a recital of how he had been lied to, and if not for the knife fight, he wouldn't have learned the truth.

"Knife fight?" Jennings said, arching an eyebrow at Fargo. He motioned at the chair in front of his desk. "Have a seat."

"Did you hear the part about him lying to me, sir?" Lieutenant Wright asked.

"I'm right here," Colonel Jennings said.

"You should hold him to account. I don't enjoy being treated like a child."

"He'd have come to see me as soon as the card game was done or he was tapped out," Colonel Jennings rightly guessed.

"You don't know that, sir," Wright said peevishly.

"I know Fargo like I know the backs of my hands, Lieutenant," Colonel Jennings said. "You can quit bitching now."

Bear River Tom laughed.

"Back to this knife business," Colonel Jennings addressed Fargo. "Who and why?"

"Beats the hell out of me," Fargo admitted. "I never set eyes on the gent before."

"Strange," Colonel Jennings said thoughtfully. "But then

it's been a strange day. It started this morning when a patrol returned with mystifying news."

"'Mystifying,'" Bear River Tom said. "There's a word you don't hear every day."

"Why are you here, exactly?" Colonel Jennings asked. "I sent for Skye, not you."

"What do you have against me?" Bear River Tom asked.

"Besides the fact that all you ever talk about is tits?"

"I will never savvy why people hold that against me," Bear River Tom said. "Seems to me tits should be as popular to talk about as the weather."

"What?" Lieutenant Wright said.

"Pay him no mind, Lieutenant," Colonel Jennings said. "He has none of his own."

"Hey, now," Bear River Tom said.

The colonel placed his forearms on his desk and clasped his hands. "As I was saying, this morning Captain Calhoun's patrol returned. I sent him to find out if there was any truth to the report I received about a new settlement in the Black Hills—"

Fargo sat up in alarm. "Hold on. Who in hell would be jackass enough to settle there?" The Black Hills were in the heart of Sioux country. The Lakotas, as they called themselves, regarded the range as sacred, and fiercely protected it.

"That's what I wanted to find out," Colonel Jennings informed him. "Captain Calhoun found the settlement, all right, which is bad enough. But what he didn't find makes it worse." Jennings paused. "No people."

"How's that again?" Fargo said.

"The settlement is there. Calhoun counted seven cabins and twice as many tents and the frame for a house. But he couldn't find a living soul."

"The Sioux got them," Bear River Tom declared. "Massacred the whole bunch."

"That was Captain Calhoun's first thought," Colonel Jennings said. "But there was no sign of a fight. No blood. No bodies. It's as if, and I'll quote him, 'every last soul up and vanished.'"

Fargo's curiosity climbed. "How many people were there?"

"Our best estimate is thirty to forty but it could be more," Colonel Jennings answered.

"How in the world did they start up a settlement without you knowing?" Bear River Tom asked.

Colonel Jennings indicated a large map on the wall behind his desk. "This Territory covers thousands of square miles. We patrol regularly but we can't be everywhere. And we can only go so far into Lakota land without risking reprisals."

"Give me a hundred men and I'd teach them to mind their betters," Lieutenant Wright spoke up.

Bear River Tom snorted. "Boy, the Sioux would eat you for breakfast. Tits or no tits."

"Hush, the both of you," Colonel Jennings commanded. "And, Tom, I won't have any more of that tit business at my fort. There are ladies here, the wives of officers and others, and if so much as one overhears you and complains, I'll throw you in the stockade and throw away the damn key. So help me God."

"It's a sad state of affairs when a man isn't free to talk about tits."

"Talk about them off my post."

"You have your army, I have my tits."

"How's that again?" Colonel Jennings said.

"You're a military man," Bear River Tom said. "You think and talk military all day long. I'm not a military man. I'm a tit man. I think and talk tits all day long. Yet people hold it against me."

"I wonder why," Colonel Jennings said. "Not another mention of tits in my presence. Understood?"

"Can I at least think tits?"

"So long as they don't leak out your mouth."

Bear River Tom frowned. "I'll try my best. But don't blame me if I slip up. Blame my mother."

Colonel Jennings drummed his fingers on the desk. "Your mother got into this how?"

"She had three."

"Three what?"

"Tits."

Fargo and the colonel and the lieutenant all stared at Bear River Tom.

"You're insane," Lieutenant Wright said.

"I sure as hell am not, pup," Bear River Tom replied. "Some ladies do. They're born with three, not two. My mother had three. It got me started on thinking about tits at an age when most boys were thinking about slingshots and fishing and such, and they've been on my mind ever since."

"Go," Colonel Jennings said, and pointed at the door.

"What?"

"You heard me. Get out of that chair and go outside and wait for Skye."

"What did I do?"

"You are the most exasperating man on the face of the planet. Whenever I talk to you, the subject always turns to tits. And it always reaches the point where I want to shout in your face to shut the hell up about tits before I shoot you."

"I thought I was the only one," Fargo said.

"You too, pard?" Bear River Tom said, sounding stricken. "I should think that you, at least, would appreciate tits more."

Colonel Jennings made a sound remarkably similar to the snort of a mad bull.

With great reluctance, Bear River Tom got up and stepped to the door. "Am I allowed the last word?"

"So long as it's not about tits," Colonel Jennings said.

Bear River Tom opened his mouth, hesitated, and closed it again. "Damn," he said, and walked out.

4

"Where the hell were we?" Colonel Jennings said.

"The missing settlers," Fargo reminded him.

"Ah, yes. I swear, that man gets me so flustered sometimes, I don't know if I'm coming or going. It's always tits, tits and more tits. Now he claims his mother had—"

"The missing settlers," Fargo said again.

"Eh?" Colonel Jennings caught himself. "Do you see? Now he has me doing it. When I go home tonight and sit across from my wife at supper, do you know what I'll be thinking of?"

"Good God, sir," Lieutenant Wright said.

"Need me to go get my bottle from my saddlebags?" Fargo asked.

Colonel Jennings shook his head. "I'm all right. But damn him, anyway. Back to these settlers." He sat up and squared his shoulders. "You can see the predicament I'm in. I'm under orders not to do anything to provoke the Lakotas. And I can't think of anything that will provoke them more than a white settlement in their sacred hills."

"So you suspect they wiped the settlers out?" Lieutenant Wright inquired.

"You did hear me mention that Captain Calhoun found no evidence of a fight? If the Sioux had attacked there would be bodies and blood and spent cartridges and broken arrows. There was none of that."

"Then what in the world happened to them, sir?"

Jennings faced Fargo. "That's what I want you to find out. You're the best scout at this post. Hell, you're one of the best scouts anywhere. I'd like you to investigate and report back to me."

"Easy to do," Fargo said.

"There's more. It could be the Sioux don't know the settlement is there, and I'd like for it to stay that way."

"How can they not know, sir?" Wright asked.

"You'd better study up on the region if you want to be an effective officer, Lieutenant," Colonel Jennings said. "The Black Hills cover five thousand square miles or more. And from what I understand, the settlement is located far from where the Sioux usually wander. And it's hidden up a gulch."

"That's something," Fargo said. He'd been to the Black Hills a number of times. The range was crisscrossed by gorges and gulches where even fifty people would be somewhat safe from the ever-watchful eyes of the Lakotas.

"I sent Captain Calhoun in discreetly, with a small force," Colonel Jennings continued. "I intend to do the same with you. I'd like you to take Lieutenant Wright and six troopers."

"Why not Calhoun?" Fargo was quick to ask. The captain was a veteran campaigner and had been in the West a good many years. He wouldn't do anything stupid. The same couldn't be said of Wright.

"I'm afraid I need him on another matter," Colonel Jennings said. "And the lieutenant can use the experience."

"I assure you, sir," Wright said, "I will be diligent in my command of this patrol—"

"You're not in charge. Fargo is."

Wright reacted as if the colonel had slapped him. "But I'm an officer. He's just a scout."

"There is nothing 'just' about him," Colonel Jennings said. "If you stayed out here fifty years, you'd be lucky to learn half of what he knows. You're to do as he says in all things. Do I make myself clear?"

"Yes, sir," Lieutenant Wright said, with the same enthusiasm he would if Jennings had told him to chop off a hand or foot.

"I mean it, Lieutenant. We can't afford mistakes. You're to slip into the Black Hills, find out what happened to those settlers, and slip out again without bringing the Sioux down on your heads."

"I won't let you down, sir," Lieutenant Wright vowed.

Jennings turned to Fargo. "There's more. I had Calhoun

do some investigating. He heard a rumor that Anton Laguerre is somehow involved."

"Who?" Wright said.

To Fargo the name was all too familiar. Laguerre was a French-Canadian as infamous in his way as Blackbeard the pirate had been in his time.

"A ruthless cutthroat," Colonel Jennings informed Wright. "Murder, thievery, rape, you name it, he's done it. He ranges all over, him and his Metis band, although this is the first I've heard of him venturing into the Black Hills."

"His what band, sir?" Wright asked.

"The Metis, Lieutenant. They hail from Canada. They're part white, part Indian. Most don't give us a lick of trouble. Laguerre and his band are the exception. They're some of the worst killers and bad men anywhere. Frankly, I can't see them wanting to have anything to do with the Black Hills. They're never involved in anything unless it can fill their pokes. But that's what Captain Calhoun was told."

Fargo was digesting all he'd been told. "None of this makes any damn sense."

"You could well have the Sioux on one hand and Laguerre on the other, and you caught in the middle," Colonel Jennings warned.

"One thing," Fargo said. "Bear River Tom will likely ask to come along. Do you mind if I take him with me?"

"Mind? By all means. And good riddance to him and his tits."

Fargo grinned.

Colonel Jennings became grimly serious. "Whatever happens out there, do me a favor and make it back alive, will you?"

"We'll sure as hell try," Fargo said.

5

True to Fargo's prediction, Tom asked to go along. He also had a brainstorm.

"We're heading out at first light, right? Then we should treat ourselves tonight."

"To what?" Fargo asked. As if he had to.

"Why, to some tits, of course. We'll pay a visit to Saucy Sally's."

Her real name was Sally Ferguson but everyone called her Saucy. The sweetest whore anywhere was how she liked to describe herself. She got her start down in New Orleans and worked the steamboats for a spell before heading upriver and somehow winding up at Fort Laramie. She'd set up a tent, hired a few of her sisters in the trade, and soon had enough money to have a log whorehouse built.

"Yes or no?" Bear River Tom prodded. "And if you say no, I'll go myself. I need some nipples to dream about over the weeks we're on the trail."

Now that Fargo thought about it, it wasn't a bad notion. He could stand to relax for a while. Once they headed out, they'd need to be on their guard every minute of every hour of every day. "Sounds fine."

Tom laughed and clapped him on the back. "I knew I could count on you. You love tits as much as I do."

"That's not possible," Fargo said.

The sign out front of the whorehouse always made him grin. Sally's Entertainment Emporium was the fancy name she had given it in order not to ruffle the feathers of the wives at the fort. The decent ladies were willing to look the other way so long as their noses weren't rubbed in the carnal cravings of their menfolk.

Fargo also grinned at the pink parlor: pink walls, pink ceiling, pink carpet, pink furnishings. A bar ran the length of the room and was tended by not one but three women in pink outfits. The novelty of female barkeeps was an attraction in its own right. Every man who visited the camp and heard about them had to come see for himself.

The doves wore pink, too: frilly, lacy, clinging pink that left little of their charms to the imagination.

If the pink wasn't enough, the perfume they wore would smother a horse. Sally was a big believer in perfume. She insisted her girls wear plenty and then sprayed it over everything else.

Fargo once asked her why she used so much and she said that she couldn't stand stink. "Crawl under the sheets with fifty or sixty smelly men a week and you won't like stink, either," was how she summed up her sentiments.

Her stable was a mix of ages and types, from Sally herself, who, it was rumored, was pushing fifty, to a couple of girls who weren't yet twenty. Blondes, brunettes, redheads, a man had his pick. Sally had also hired a black gal and a Chinese girl because, as she put it, "Blacks and Asians got peckers, too."

No sooner did Fargo and Bear River Tom stride in than there was a lusty whoop of delight and a pink tent on two thick legs waddled toward them with her thick arms spread wide.

"Skye! Thomas! How are two of my favorite gentlemen in all the world?"

When Sally hugged you, Fargo had discovered, it was like being hugged by a bear. It was a wonder his ribs didn't stave in. That they didn't was because they were cushioned by breasts roughly the size of Conestogas. Sally had the hugest breasts he'd ever seen, and that took some doing. They were so huge, he marveled that she could bend over without falling on her face.

"You get a hug, too, you rascal, you," Sally said, and turned to Tom.

"Sweet Sally," Bear River Tom said. He looked to be in heavenly rapture as they embraced. "You don't know how much I've missed these tits of yours."

"You can tell me all about it in a while," Sally said with a playful wink. "But before we get to that, how about a drink on the house and you boys tell ol' Sal what you've been up to?"

" 'On the house' are three of my favorite words," Fargo said.

Sally pulled them toward a sofa. Several girls were there, waiting to be picked, and she shooed them away and sank down in the middle. "Have a seat, fellas."

Fargo was amazed the sofa didn't buckle. He sat on her left and had to wriggle to fit, she took up so much room. "How's business, Saucy?"

"Never better."

Fargo surveyed the revelers and realized something. "I don't see as many boys in blue as usual."

"They've had to cut back on their visits for the time being," Sally confided. "A few of them snuck away from the fort last week to pay me a visit, and they were on duty at the time. So that colonel of theirs clamped down."

"That's a shame," Bear River Tom said. "You have good tits here."

"I do like girls on the busty side," Sally said.

Bear River Tom placed a hand on one of hers and said sadly, "A tit is a terrible thing to waste."

"You're a beautiful man, Thomas," Saucy Sally said. "For that you get to have me free."

"Hot damn," Tom said.

"If one tit is a waste," Fargo tried, "two tits are a calamity."

Both Tom and Sally swiveled to stare at him.

"I'm sorry," she said. "That won't earn you a free poke. You're just copying Tom."

"I'm a beautiful man," Bear River Tom said proudly.

"You're something," Fargo said.

Sally raised her arms and clapped her hands and one of the lady barkeeps sashayed over, her hips swinging wide.

Sally told her to bring a bottle of their finest whiskey and three glasses.

"Tall glasses," Fargo said.

"That's Rebecca," Sally said as the girl sashayed back. "You might like her, Skye." She chuckled and jabbed him with her elbow.

Fargo had to admit he was interested. Rebecca was one of

the young ones, with auburn hair and green eyes and the kind of full lips he liked to suck on. "You've got her tending bar."

"I can pull her away for a while," Sally said. "I'm her boss, remember?"

When Rebecca returned bearing a tray with their drinks, Sally crooked a finger and said something in her ear.

Rebecca nodded and smiled and stepped in front of Fargo. A twinkle in her emerald eyes, she huskily remarked, "I hear you'd like to poke me."

Fargo stared at the junction of her thighs and his mouth watered. "Would I ever," he said.

6

Her room was typical of those at Saucy Sally's—small and to the point. There was a bed and a table with a lamp and an incense burner. The scents varied. This one smelled of lilacs.

Rebecca closed the door and stood with her back to it and her right knee crooked so that her dress clung to her thigh. "You were saying?"

More often than not Fargo liked to make love slow and easy but this night was different. He couldn't say why he wanted to take her hard and fast. Maybe it was the thought of what lay ahead. Mortality, a wise man once claimed, lent a sweet savor to life.

Pressing his chest to her breasts and his thighs to hers, he said in her ear, "I'll let my hands do my talking."

Rebecca looked down, and grinned. "Your hands and something else, I see." She slid a hand between them. "Oh, my. Hard already? You must really want me."

"I want you to shut up," Fargo said, and ensured she did by covering her mouth with his.

Rebecca was good. She had talent. When she kissed, she moved her lips in light little nibbles and rimmed his teeth. She sucked on his tongue and moaned when he sucked on hers.

Fargo's hands were as busy as his mouth. He ran his right hand up and down her thigh while covering a breast with his left. When he pinched her nipple through her dress she quaked with desire.

Some women showed no more feeling at being caressed than a lump of clay. They hardly ever made a sound or let their longing get the better of them. Not Rebecca. She was a violin eager to be played.

Fargo hiked at her dress and was delighted to find she had nothing on underneath. Chemises and petticoats were fine but they tended to delay things and tonight he didn't care to waste a moment. Which was why his hand delved to her slit and his finger parted her silken smooth wetness.

"Ohhh," Rebecca husked in his ear. "No beating around the bush for you."

"Not when it's as nice as yours," Fargo said.

"Flattery, you handsome devil," Rebecca said, "will get you everywhere."

Fargo pressed his thumb to her tiny knob. "Ready or not," he said. His pole was a ramrod, his blood boiled with need. Spreading her legs, he positioned himself between them.

"What about the bed?" she asked.

"What about it?" Fargo rejoined, and impaled himself to the hilt, as it were, with a hard thrust that brought him up onto the tips of his toes.

"God in heaven!" Rebecca exclaimed, throwing back her head. "There's so much of you."

Fargo kissed her as she wrapped her winsome legs around his waist and locked her ankles at the small of his back. He cupped her bottom to support her weight. Not that she weighed much. Unlike Sally, she was tits and ass and not much else.

Dipping at the knees, he thrust up and in. She gasped as he went on doing so, each time harder and faster than the time before, until soon he was slamming into her like a steam engine piston and she was puffing and huffing like a racehorse that had run a mile.

They both rapidly climbed to the brink. Rebecca crested first, and to her credit, there were none of the telltale signs that she was faking it, as a lot of girls did. When she came, she came, spurting and contracting and bringing a constriction to his throat with his own impending eruption.

"Now," she breathed. "Oh, now."

Fargo let himself go. They were thumping against the wall loud enough to be heard in the parlor but he didn't give a damn.

They thumped quite a while. Finally Fargo coasted to a stop and Rebecca sagged against him with her cheek to his chest.

"That was nice."

"Aren't they all?"

"No," Rebecca said. "A lot of men are clumsy and awkward or lumps of clay."

Fargo had heard her lament before. The truth be known, he wasn't fond of lumps, himself. A woman who didn't like to make love shouldn't waste the man's time.

Rebecca started to lower her legs.

Firming his hold, he turned and carried her to the bed and gently deposited her on her back, then stretched out next to her.

"How about a second helping in a minute or two?" he asked.

"That soon?"

"Bear River Tom and his damn tit talk has me randy as hell," Fargo admitted.

Rebecca laughed. "He does tend to go on about them, doesn't he?"

"There's no 'tend' about it," Fargo said. "He lives and breathes tit."

"Did you know he asked Sally to marry him?"

Fargo stared at her.

"I'm serious. He told her that she has the biggest he's ever seen and he'd like to spend the rest of his days with them in his mouth."

"That sounds like Tom."

"He's fun in bed, she says. He has more ways of making love to her tits than any john she's done."

"That sounds like Tom, too."

"She almost said yes. She's not getting any younger and she thinks he meant it when he told her he'd take care of her and her tits as if they were made of gold."

Fargo snorted. "Romantic cuss."

"What would you compare my tits to? If hers are gold, what are mine?"

"Tits," Fargo said.

"I was fishing for a compliment. A girl likes to be appreciated."

"How about this," Fargo said, and nuzzled her neck. "You're a great lay."

"That will have to do, I suppose," Rebecca said, and giggled.

That was when the door burst open and the man with the eye patch and the scar came at Fargo in a rush.

7

It was the same man dressed in the same clothes, and something about them pricked at Fargo's memory. The thought was there and it was gone.

He barely had time to react. Cold steel flashed at his neck, and he rolled.

Rebecca screamed. She scrambled back as the knife missed her by inches.

Fargo still had his pants on but they were undone, and when he shoved the small man back and leaped off the bed, they started to slide down his legs. Retreating, he got them up and buckled.

He grabbed for his Colt but his attacker was on him, cutting at his hand to keep him from drawing.

Fargo kneed him in the balls.

Most hombres, that would end the fight. Not this one.

The small man snarled and stabbed at his throat.

Fargo barely got his arm up to deflect the man's wrist. He drove his fist into the other's jaw but it didn't flatten him as he hoped. It only made him madder.

Again Fargo grabbed for his Colt. He had the six-shooter half out when a blow to his wrist numbed his hand. The man with the eye patch stabbed at his chest and he sidestepped.

The man's momentum carried him a half step past and close to the bed.

Rebecca did a remarkable thing. Lunging, she raked the man's face with her fingernails.

The man swore and skipped back.

Fargo went to pounce but a sweep of that glittering blade held him at bay.

Rebecca had drawn blood. Scarlet streaks marked the

man's forehead and some were trickling into his good eye. Shaking his head, he growled in anger and abruptly wheeled and bounded from the room.

Fargo went after him. He tried to draw but his hand was still numb and his thumb and forefinger wouldn't work as they should.

The man raced to the rear. He hit the back door on the fly and spilled out into the night.

Fargo exploded out after him. He glimpsed the small figure melting into the darkness and gave chase. Within twenty feet he'd lost sight of him. Stopping, he listened for footfalls. There were none.

His attacker might have gone to ground.

Fargo roved in a circle but no luck. He roved wider. He was on his third circle when Bear River Tom pounded from the whorehouse shirtless and holding his revolver.

"Where are you, hoss?"

"Over here," Fargo grumbled. He was annoyed at himself for letting the man get away.

"Rebecca came running into Sally's room, hollering about a man trying to kill you."

"This makes twice now."

"The same Metis from the saloon?"

Fargo almost smacked his forehead. The killer's small cap, those clothes. The man was one of the French-Canadians with Indian blood who came south each summer to hunt buffalo and trade with the Indian tribes.

"What's the matter?" Bear River Tom asked. "You look surprised."

"I should have seen it sooner."

"Strange, though, isn't it?"

"That he keeps trying to kill me and I have no notion why?"

"That he's one of those mixed-blood Frenchers. The same as Anton Laguerre."

"Son of a bitch," Fargo said.

8

A blaze of orange and red filled the eastern sky with the rising of the sun.

Fort Laramie roused to life. A bugler played reveille and presently troopers hustled from the barracks to line up for morning roll call, many struggling to shake off sleep.

Fargo was doing some struggling himself. He'd spent the night with Rebecca and downed almost a full bottle of Monongahela before he fell asleep. She had him feeling stiff and sore and the whiskey had him feeling sluggish, to boot, as he led the Ovaro by the reins to the headquarters building.

Bear River Tom was his usual vinegar-and-vim self. "Look at that sunrise, pard. It's almost as glorious as Saucy Sally's tits."

"Don't start," Fargo warned. "I don't want to hear another word about tits before noon."

"You expect me not to talk tits for six whole hours?"

Colonel Jennings emerged with the orderly in tow. "Did I just hear the word 'tits'?"

"You did not," Bear River Tom said.

The colonel looked Fargo up and down and said, "You look like something the cat dragged in."

"Good morning to you, too," Fargo said.

"You have to forgive him, Colonel," Bear River Tom said. "He got up on the wrong side of a whore's bed this morning."

"That will be enough about whores, thank you," Colonel Jennings said. "You never know who might be listening."

"I can't talk tits and I can't talk about whores." Bear River Tom sighed. "What is this world coming to?"

"Where the dickens is Lieutenant Wright?" Colonel Jennings said. "I told him to be here at the crack of dawn."

24

"Isn't that him yonder?" Bear River Tom asked, pointing.

At the far end of the parade ground, near the stable, Wright and six troopers were climbing on their mounts. The last man held the lead rope to a pair of pack animals.

Fargo squinted, trying to make out their faces. "Did you pick men with experience or do I have to hold their hands?"

"That's hardly fair," Colonel Jennings. "Except for a few senior officers like myself and a couple of sergeants, my command is made up of recruits fresh off the farm or city boys. The army expects me to make soldiers of them and I do the best I can."

"Hold their hands it is," Fargo said.

"You need only hold Wright's and he'll hold theirs," Jennings said. "We call that the chain of command."

"I call it asking for trouble," Fargo said.

Bear River Tom nodded. "It's plain dumb to send infants into Lakota country. We run into a war party, there's not a damn one of them who'll make it back to this fort alive."

"I'm counting on Fargo and you to see that they do," Jennings said.

Fargo would do his best but he wasn't a miracle worker. The truth was, most boys in blue were poor shots and fair riders. None of which was their fault.

The army pinched pennies everywhere it could, and that included ammunition. If they were lucky, troopers got to fire half a dozen rounds once a month. That hardly made marksmen out of them. It didn't help that the army issued single-shot rifles instead of repeaters since repeaters cost more.

Parade drill was daily, and often on horseback, but walking a horse through its paces on a flat parade ground couldn't compare to riding rugged terrain in the wilds. A lot of troopers rode about as well as a ten-year-old Sioux.

"Here they come," Bear River Tom said.

"Do you see that third man in line?" Colonel Jennings asked.

Fargo looked. The "man" was all of eighteen if he was a day, with curly blond hair and a baby face. "The one in diapers?"

"I wouldn't say that around him, were I you," Colonel Jennings said. "That's General Davenport's son."

25

"Blood and Guts Davenport?" Bear River Tom said. "I know that old he-bull. Any harm comes to his pride and joy, he'll have us skinned alive."

"All the more reason not to let anything happen to Oleandar," Colonel Jennings said.

"Who?"

"Oleandar Winston Davenport. Private Davenport to you."

"Good God," Bear River Tom said. "Who names a boy Oleandar? That's almost as bad as naming him Tits."

Colonel Jennings glared.

"What?" Tom said.

"My sources tell me his mother named him and the general went along with her as he does with most anything she wants. He cracks the whip in the army but she cracks the whip at home."

"Oleandar," Bear River Tom said, and laughed. "If my ma had named me that, I'd chuck her off a cliff."

"Why not leave the general's boy here?" Fargo suggested. The last thing he needed was a general mad at him.

"Young Davenport has to acquire experience somehow," Jennings said.

"Can't acquire much when you're dead," Bear River Tom remarked.

"He's going and that's final."

Lieutenant Wright drew rein and saluted snappily. "Reporting for duty as ordered, sir."

"At ease, Lieutenant," Colonel Jennings said. "I trust you remember what I told you about Fargo being in charge?"

"I'd rather he wasn't, sir, but I always do as I'm ordered."

Colonel Jennings surprised Fargo by stepping around the hitch rail and offering his hand. "Just in case."

"Don't sugarcoat it," Bear River Tom said. "Come right out and tell him you think he's a gone gosling. Hell, that all of us are."

"Get him out of here," Jennings said.

"Why are you always picking on me?" Tom asked.

Fargo forked leather. Reining around, he tapped his spurs and didn't look back. Once clear of the post, he swung to the north. He figured to cover a lot of miles before sundown.

Bear River Tom brought his roan alongside the Ovaro. "Pick a number between one and nine."

"Go annoy someone else," Fargo said.

"I've got ten dollars that says only two of us make it back alive and you can guess which two."

"Keep that to yourself."

"You don't want me spooking the little boy bluebellies? Don't worry, pard. I'll let them learn the truth the hard way." Tom paused. "By dying."

9

When most folks in the East thought of the prairie, they imagined a vast flat sea of waving grass. While there were stretches like that, more often the lay of the land consisted of rolling hills and rises bisected by canyons and washes or towered over by buttes and bluffs.

Grass of different kinds was plentiful but there was also mesquite and the thistle that broke off in strong winds to become tumbleweed and wildflowers and milkweed and clover and wild onion and more. In certain areas at certain times of the year there were sunflowers and coneflowers and plantain and black-eyed Susans.

With such a great feast of plant life, it followed that there was an abundance of wildlife. The huge herds of buffalo were the animals most people thought of when someone mentioned the prairie, but the buffs were but one of many. Deer and a few elk and antelope called the prairie home, too, as did wolves and coyotes and foxes and cougars and a host of lesser animals on which they fed.

It amused Fargo no end that one of the first white men to explore west of the Mississippi River had told everyone it was nothing but a "great desert." He had to wonder if the man rode around with his eyes closed.

He was reminded of it when, on their second day out of Fort Laramie, Lieutenant Archibald Wright brought his sorrel up to pace him and remarked, "If there is anything more boring than this godforsaken prairie, I have yet to come across it."

Fargo watched a red hawk wheel high in the sky and heard a sharp whistle and saw prairie dogs scamper down their holes.

"I could never be a scout," Wright said. "I couldn't take this boredom."

In the distance antelope took flight in long, graceful bounds.

"How do you manage?" Wright asked.

"I reckon I just like a dull life," Fargo said.

Lieutenant Wright looked at him and seemed to be contemplating, and then said, "Tell me something. Is it true what Bear River Tom told me, that you lived with the Sioux once?"

"For a short spell," Fargo confirmed. He'd also lived with the Apaches and others.

"How could you? I mean, given the fact they're Indians?"

"They're people," Fargo said, "like us."

"The hell they are," Wright said. "White and red are as different as night and day. They're savages, for God's sake."

"And what are we?"

"What kind of question is that? We're civilized. We have laws and government and culture. What do they have?"

"Tribal councils and chiefs and what you call a culture all their own."

"Be serious. They run around in animal hides and disport themselves like animals."

"Disport?" Fargo said.

"You know what I mean. They're heathens. They don't believe in God like we do."

"Ah."

"Ah what? Don't tell me that when you lived with them you took up their heathen ways?"

"Ever hear of the Great Spirit?" Fargo asked.

"That hogwash the Indians believe in? Yes, the colonel told us about it and said we should try to respect their beliefs if we're to get along with them."

"Jennings is a good man."

"If you ask me, he's too weak-kneed," Wright said. "The Sioux hate us. They don't want to get along with us. They want to drive us out."

"They were here long before we were."

"So you're one of *those*," Wright said. "In that case let me make my own feelings clear. I don't care that they were here first. We're here now, and all this land will one day be ours. We owe it to the settlers who are flocking to the West to make it a decent place to live by keeping the hostiles in check by any means necessary."

"You'd put them all on reservations, I bet."

"Of course. Or exterminate those who refuse to go. That's what you do with vermin."

Fargo controlled his temper enough to say, "There's a lot of hate on both sides. And a lot of stupid."

"Are you referring to me?"

"If the boot fits."

"I don't like being insulted. To be honest, the more I get to know of you, the less I understand why Colonel Jennings admires you so." Wright wheeled his mount and rejoined his men.

Not half a minute later Bear River Tom took his place. "What did you say to get the lieutenant's britches up around his nose? He's back there ready to spit nails."

"He's a jackass."

"You know why, don't you?"

"Don't start," Fargo warned.

"He didn't squeeze enough tits growing up. The more tits a man squeezes, the more mature he is."

"Do you ever listen to yourself?"

"I never talk to myself, no," Tom said. "You have to be loco to do that."

Fargo glanced behind them at the troopers, and stiffened. Half a mile or so back there was a bright flash of light. It was there and it was gone. The kind of flash caused by, say, the sun glinting off metal.

"What?" Bear River Tom said, and shifted in his saddle. "I don't see anything."

"It could be we're being followed."

"Hostiles, you reckon?"

"This soon?" Fargo rejoined. He deemed it unlikely that a war party would venture so close to the fort.

"We'll have to find out who. Do you want to flip a coin to see who goes?"

"Me," Fargo said.

"Why you?"

"I'm in charge."

"So you get to have fun and I get stuck with the green bluebellies?"

"You'll be a fine nursemaid."

"Just so I don't have to change their diapers."

10

Fargo let another mile go by before he made his move. They had just crested a low hill when he slowed to let Lieutenant Wright come up. "I'm dropping back. Keep going with Tom and I'll catch up."

"Why are you leaving us?"

Fargo saw no harm in saying, "I think we're being shadowed."

"By who?"

"I won't know until I see them." Fargo lifted his reins to go.

"Hold on. You should take a couple of my men with you."

"No."

"To back you up."

"I don't need backing."

"It's common sense. What if there are more than one? What if something happens to you?"

"I'll be fine."

"If you ask me," Wright said, "you're too smug by half. I know you don't think highly of us but we're not incompetent."

Fargo almost said, "You're damn close to it." Instead, he replied, "You give orders a lot better than you take them. The colonel said you're to do as I say."

"Nice of you to remind me every chance you get," Wright said. "But very well. And if we never see you again, I'll put it in my report that you died due to your own pigheadedness."

The troopers looked quizzically at Fargo as he rode past.

Private Oleandar Davenport smiled and looked as if he was about to say something but didn't.

Fargo put them from his mind for the time being. He circled around the hill and stopped when he could see their

32

back trail. Dismounting, he shucked his Henry from the saddle scabbard.

A small boulder a stone's throw up the slope was the only cover. It would have to do. He climbed and flattened and took off his hat. Folding his arms, he rested his chin on his wrist and settled down to wait. It shouldn't be long, he reckoned.

It wasn't.

A lone rider appeared, coming on at a walk. Fargo wasn't at all surprised to see who it was.

The killer with the eye patch rode with the casual air of someone at home in the wilds. There was none of the nervousness of the young soldiers. His good eye was bent to the ground, and he held his reins loosely. A rifle butt poked from a scabbard, and he had his knife on his hip.

It annoyed Fargo that Tom had realized the man was a Metis before he had. He couldn't afford lapses like that. They too often proved fatal.

Sliding the Henry past the boulder, he tucked the stock to his shoulder and took a bead. Shooting from ambush didn't bother him, not when the bastard had tried twice to kill him.

Instead of aiming at the head or the heart, though, he centered the Henry's sights on the man's shoulder. He'd like to take him alive and ask a few questions.

The Metis raised his head and regarded the hill, and just like that he reined sharply around and jabbed his heels against his bay.

Fargo swore. The same thing that had given the Metis away earlier—the flash of sunlight off metal—had now given him away. The Henry's brass receiver must have caught the sun just right. He banged off a shot but was sure he missed. Jacking the lever, he pushed to his knees and went to fire again.

Well out from the hill, the Metis performed a feat worthy of a Sioux warrior; he swung onto the side of his bay, hanging by a foot over its back and an arm over its neck.

Fargo aimed at the foot. He might hit the horse but it couldn't be helped. Just as his finger began to tighten, horse and rider disappeared. It was as if the earth swallowed them.

Grabbing his hat, Fargo raced down the hill to the Ovaro.

He vaulted into the saddle, hauled on the reins and used his spurs.

A gully explained how the Metis had vanished.

Fargo galloped down into it and along its winding course to where it opened into a stretch of flat prairie. Beyond were hills.

The Metis and the bay were nowhere to be seen.

Fargo made for the hills. He spotted tracks and leaned down for a closer look. The whistle of lead and the crack of a rifle were simultaneous.

Wheeling the Ovaro, Fargo galloped for the gully. The rifle cracked a second time and a slug missed his head, but not by much. Fear spiked in him that the Metis might try to bring down the Ovaro, and he cut right and then left.

He reached the gully and sprang down. Moving to the rim, he scanned the hills. The man with the eye patch had to be somewhere on the nearest, but if so, he was well hid.

Fargo felt a certain begrudging respect. Whoever this small man was, he was damn good.

Fargo stayed put, hoping the killer would show himself. He got his wish but not in the manner he expected.

The bay and its rider appeared atop the second hill, not the first. Safely out of range, the man with the eye patch raised an arm as if in salute, then turned his animal and rode down the far side.

"I'll be damned," Fargo said. His respect climbed. This Metis had a flair about him.

Reluctantly, Fargo shoved the Henry into the scabbard and climbed back on the Ovaro. He didn't give chase. It would be pointless. The Metis had too great a lead, and something told him that bay would prove to possess as much stamina as the Ovaro.

Something also told him he hadn't seen the last of them. Sooner or later, that small man with the eye patch would try again.

11

Lieutenant Wright was a stickler for the manual. He posted a sentry by the horse string even though the horses weren't twenty feet from their campfire. The troopers were to take turns standing watch.

"One good thing about having these kids along," Bear River Tom remarked to Fargo, "is we get to have a good night's sleep."

Fargo doubted he'd rest all that easy. Not with the Metis out there somewhere, and liable to sneak in and try to slit his throat in the dead of night.

"I heard that," Lieutenant Wright said, taking a seat across from them. "And I'll thank you to stop calling my men 'kids.'"

"Sorry, sonny," Bear River Tom said. "But when you're not old enough to shave, that's what you are."

"I'll have you know I shave twice a week whether I need to or not."

"That often, huh?"

Wright focused on Fargo. "Tell me more about this one-eyed killer."

"You know as much as I do."

"Which is nothing," Wright said. "You're supposed to be one of the best plainsmen alive. How could he get away from you?"

"It happens," Fargo said.

"I hate to think we'll have him on our trail all the way to the Black Hills," Wright complained. "Surely you can come up with a way to catch him."

"I'm working on it."

"What I don't savvy," Bear River Tom said, "is how the

Metis are involved with those settlers who have gone missing."

Neither did Fargo. The Metis rarely visited towns or settlements. Considered outcasts because of their mixed blood, they kept to themselves. They dealt more with the Indians than with whites, trading for hides and sometimes plunder. But according to Captain Calhoun's report to the colonel, the settlement hadn't been raided.

"So much for the great scouts," Lieutenant Wright remarked.

"Keep it up, sonny," Bear River Tom said, "and you'll be eating teeth."

"Anytime you want to try, tit fiend, feel free," Lieutenant Wright said.

Tom blinked. "What did you just call me?"

"Tit fiend," Fargo said.

"That I did," Wright said. "And it's only fair to warn you that I was the top of my class in the fine art of boxing."

"A scrawny runt like you?" Bear River Tom scoffed.

Lieutenant Wright jumped to his feet and raised his fists. "I'll thrash you here and now if you dare try me."

"Sit down," Fargo said.

"I will not." Wright moved around the fire until he was only a step away from Tom. "I've had enough of you two looking down your noses at me. I challenge this lout to a fight."

"Now, Archibald . . ." Tom said with a smirk.

"Archibald *this*," Wright snapped, and stabbed the toe of his left boot at the ground. Dirt flew up, not a lot, but it caught Bear River Tom flush in the face, causing him to turn his face away.

"You damned pup."

"Stand and fight."

Fargo was dumbfounded, and he wasn't the only one. The troopers sitting a few yards away were slack-jawed and wide-eyed.

"Lieutenant," Private Davenport made bold to say, "what on earth has gotten into you?"

"I have been belittled long enough," Wright said without looking at him. "And you and the others will keep silent and not interfere. Is that understood?" He gestured at Tom. "On your feet, bumpkin."

"First I'm a tit fiend and now I'm a bumpkin. Make up your puny mind."

"I'll show you puny," Lieutenant Wright said.

Bear River Tom turned to Fargo. "It's up to you, pard. Can I or can't I?"

"You can," Fargo said.

Bear River Tom set down his rifle and rose. He stood a good head and shoulders over the lieutenant and outweighed him by at least fifty pounds, but Wright didn't seem to care. "Boy, I've whipped bigger men than you without half trying."

"You'll have to try with me," Wright said. "Raise your fists and defend yourself."

"I don't go in for that fancy stuff," Bear River Tom said. "Whenever you want this dance to commence, get to hopping."

"Don't expect me to go easy on you just because you're ignorant of the science of fisticuffs."

"You know where you can shove your science, boy?"

"Stop calling me *boy*," Lieutenant Wright cried, and waded in with his bony fists flying.

Bear River Tom just stood there. A left connected with his cheek and a right whipped into his stomach. All he did was wince. "Is that the best you can do?"

Archibald Wright lost control. With a half growl, half scream, he waded in again.

Tom got an arm up but he didn't make any great effort to avoid the rain of blows. He grunted when an uppercut clipped his jaw and again when Wright slammed him in the ribs. When Wright stepped back, he was the one breathing heavily.

"Not bad, youngster," Bear River Tom said, rubbing his side. "Some of them stung."

Wright looked at his fists and then at Tom. "This can't be. What are you made of?"

"Flesh and bone, boy."

"I told you to stop calling me that." Wright sprang and cocked his right arm but before the blow could land, Bear River Tom unleashed a backhand that caught Wright full in the face and knocked him flat on his back.

"Stay down, pup," Tom said. "I don't want to hurt you."

Rubbing his chin, Wright looked up in amazement. "I hit you with all I had."

"It's not how a man hits," Tom said, "it's how much he can take." He extended his hand. "Here. I'll help you up."

Anger and bewilderment had Wright confused. He let himself be pulled to his feet, and shook his head. "I've never been so humiliated."

"You've got nothing to be ashamed of," Bear River Tom said. "Give yourself a few years and you'll be someone to be reckoned with."

"Don't patronize me."

"Hell, I don't even know what that means." Tom chuckled and clapped the lieutenant on the arm. "I'm only saying that tough trumps everything else. Look at the Apaches. Or look at him." Tom pointed at Fargo.

"Are you saying he's tougher than you?"

"Fargo there is the toughest son of a bitch I know, and that's saying a lot. If you'd pulled your stunt with him, you'd be spitting teeth."

Wright frowned and his shoulders slumped. "I've been made a fool of in front of my men."

"That's one way of looking at it."

"What's another?"

"That you learned an important lesson," Bear River Tom said. "A man has to know his limits. Now you know yours like I know mine."

"What about him?" Wright asked with a nod at Fargo. "What are his limits?"

"He doesn't have any."

Wright scowled and said, "He doesn't seem so formidable to me."

"Take a swing at him, then," Bear River Tom said, "and see what happens."

Lieutenant Archibald Wright stared into Fargo's eyes and slowly shook his head. "No, I don't believe I will. I need these teeth to chew my food."

Bear River Tom grinned. "There's hope for you yet, Archie."

12

The fight took a lot of the starch out of Lieutenant Wright. Over the next several days he was a lot friendlier. To Fargo and Bear River Tom, anyway. To his men he was still a no-nonsense officer who barked his orders and took them to task if they didn't keep their uniforms clean.

Right there was one of the reasons Fargo had never joined the regular army. He couldn't abide being bossed around. He could abide it even less when the things he was told to do were downright stupid.

He did love scouting. He got to do what he enjoyed most, wandering all over creation. And he was paid for it. That, and he didn't have to wear a uniform and was pretty much left alone when his talents weren't needed.

Those talents served him in good stead now. Two days after the fight, he cut the sign of a party of seven warriors. The troopers would never have noticed. Unless tracks were as plain as the noses on their faces, the boys in blue might as well be blind. But Fargo noticed. So did Bear River Tom.

They dismounted and were studying them when their new bosom friend asked, "What is it? What do you see?"

"Injuns," Bear River Tom answered. "Seven, if my count is right." He looked at Fargo.

Fargo nodded. "Could be a hunting party. Could be a war party." He pointed. "They're heading north."

"Sioux?" Lieutenant Wright asked.

"Could be," Fargo said again. "We can't tell by the hoof-prints."

"All we know is the horses weren't shod and there were seven of them," Bear River Tom amplified.

"How you can tell anything is a marvel to me," Wright admitted. "All I see is some crushed grass and scuff marks."

"The ground is hard," Bear River Tom said. "We could do with some rain."

That they could, Fargo reflected. Thunderstorms were fairly common at that time of year but so far the sky had stayed clear and virtually cloudless. Which was too bad. A downpour would wipe out their own tracks and help hide them from the Sioux.

Lieutenant Wright's saddle creaked as he turned. "Do you think that one-eyed man is still stalking us?"

"Why would he stop?" Fargo said. "He hasn't done what he set out to do."

"Which is to kill you, for some reason," Wright said. "But why you and not, say, Tom, here?"

"Hey, now," Tom said, "why would anyone want to kill me?"

"I heard Colonel Jennings say that he would like to. It had something to do with tits."

"Well, hell," Tom said.

Fargo stayed alert for dust and smoke and anything else that would forewarn them of hostiles.

They were raising dust, themselves. Not a lot. Not so much that the Sioux would notice, he hoped.

That evening, as the troopers sat clustered around the fire and Fargo sat honing his Arkansas toothpick on a whetstone, someone coughed to get his attention. Thinking it was Wright, he looked up.

"Sorry to disturb you," Private Oleandar Davenport said. "I thought it was time I introduced myself."

"I know who you are," Fargo said. "And I know your pa, the general."

"He's spoken very highly of you," Private Davenport mentioned.

Fargo stared at the younger man's uniform where insignia would be. "Why a private?"

"I've only been in the army a short while."

"No," Fargo said. "Why aren't you following in his footsteps?"

"Oh. That." Davenport looked away. "My father and I argued over that, actually. He wanted me to do as he did and attend officer's school and start my career as a lieutenant, like Lieutenant Wright has done."

"That's how most would do it."

"I don't want it to be easier for me than it is for most everyone else."

Fargo didn't understand. "From what I hear, West Point is hard as hell to get through."

"But if you make it you're automatically an officer."

"What's wrong with that?"

"I consider it the same as having my life handed to me on a silver platter. I'd much rather do it the ordinary way. The way most men do."

"You'd rather take orders than give them?"

"It's not that," Davenport said. "All my life I've been treated as if I'm special just because I'm General Davenport's son."

"What's wrong with that?" Fargo asked once more.

"I don't want to be treated special. I want to be treated like everyone else."

"Why?"

"Because it's not fair that an accident of birth places me above them."

"Most men would give anything to be in your boots."

"That doesn't make it right. Our common brotherhood demands the same opportunities for all."

"Your common what?"

"Deep down, all men are brothers. We share a common heritage. Life itself."

"Where the hell did you get that from?"

"I've given it a lot of thought over the years," Davenport said. His face clouded. "My father calls me immature, if you can believe it."

"You are."

"I beg your pardon?"

"The only brothers a man has are those his mother gives birth to."

"I beg to disagree. Surely you've heard that we're each our brother's keeper?"

"You should be a parson," Fargo said.

"That wouldn't prove anything to my father." Private

Davenport plucked at his sleeve. "This will. I wear it to show him I'm willing to live just as he did, but by the principles I believe in, not his."

"That's fine and dandy," Fargo said. "Just so you're willing to die for them, too."

13

The next morning they were up at the crack of dawn and under way before the sun was up.

Fargo hadn't gone two hundred yards when he drew rein. There, in a patch of dirt, was the clear imprint of a shod hoof. Climbing down, he examined it. As near as he could judge, it wasn't an hour old.

"A lone white man, this close to our camp?" Lieutenant Wright said when he was informed. "Was he spying on us?"

"Stay put," Fargo said. On foot he backtracked the rider. Most of the prints were partials or scrapes but he found enough to show that the rider had circled their camp, staying well out, and then had gone off in the direction they were headed, toward the Black Hills.

"So he *was* spying on us," Lieutenant Wright said.

"My money is on Skye's one-eyed friend," Bear River Tom guessed.

"He's ahead of us now?" Wright said.

"And in a hurry, too," Fargo told him. The spacing between prints revealed the one-eyed man had brought his bay to a trot as soon as he was out of earshot.

"Well, at least we won't have to worry about him being behind us anymore," Wright said.

"He can shoot us from the front as easy as from the back," Bear River Tom mentioned.

But the rest of the day proved uneventful. As did the day after that, and the next.

The young troopers became used to the heat and long hours in the saddle and their pale skins became red and then bronzed from the sun.

It was about two hundred miles from Fort Laramie to the Black Hills. Fargo went easy to spare wear on the horses, and because the troopers were so green. They managed twenty to twenty-five miles a day.

Nine days after setting out they drew rein on the crest of a grassy ridge and beheld a dark spine in the distance.

"At last," Bear River Tom said.

"Those are the Black Hills?" Lieutenant Wright said. "They look more like mountains."

"They are," Fargo said. To the best of his recollection, the highest peak was over a mile high. Most, though, were considerably less. The reason the range appeared so dark and why they were called the Black Hills became apparent once they were nearer.

"Look at all the trees, sir," Private Davenport marveled.

The change was striking, from rolling grassland to thick timber broken by rocky heights. And every square foot of it sacred to the Sioux.

According to Colonel Jennings, the gulch the settlers picked was along the northwest edge of the range. Fargo hoped that worked in their favor in that the Lakotas were less likely to be this far out.

They were skirting the bottoms of the forested slopes when Bear River Tom pointed at the ground and said, "Lookee there, pard."

Wagon tracks, old ones, the ruts worn shallow by rain and wind.

"The settlers," Bear River Tom said. "It has to be. All we have to do is follow them and they'll take us right where we need to go."

The homesteaders had chosen well. The mouth of the gulch was hidden from the outlying prairie by a spur of forest. It was only because the ruts brought them right to the opening that they realized it was there.

"I'll be damned," Lieutenant Wright said. "Quite clever of them, wouldn't you agree?"

Almost too clever, Fargo mused. Judging by how the wagons had made a beeline for the gulch, the settlers hadn't stumbled on it by accident.

The gulch widened. A small stream gurgled to their left.

Beyond rose forest, a mix of pine and juniper and mahogany. To the right reared granite spires and cliffs.

The sun glistening on the water, the green of the pines, the frolicking sparrows and squawking jays, prompted Bear River Tom to remark, "It's downright pretty here."

"No wonder they liked it," Lieutenant Wright said.

They rode around a bend and then another, and suddenly the pretty aspects melted away like so much dew.

In the shadow of a great granite cliff, cabins and tents lined the stream's bank. The tent flaps hung limp while most of the cabin doors were wide-open. There wasn't a living soul to be seen. Here and there lay scattered possessions: a dish, a torn blanket, a shirt.

"This is plumb strange," Bear River Tom said.

"We should call out," Lieutenant Wright said, putting a hand to his mouth.

"Sound carries a long ways," Fargo warned. "The quieter we are, the less chance the Sioux will find us."

"Sorry. I wasn't thinking."

Alighting, Fargo yanked his Henry from the scabbard. "Have your men spread out and search every cabin, every tent."

"Captain Calhoun reported the place to be deserted."

"It can't hurt to check again," Fargo said. Especially for sign of recent visitors.

Bear River Tom was the last to climb down. "I have a spooky feeling, pard."

"Since when did you become superstitious?" Fargo asked.

"I laugh at rabbits' feet and four-leaf clovers, true," Bear River Tom said. "This is different." He gazed the length of the settlement. "I think we're being watched."

Fargo had experienced the same sensation from time to time but he didn't have it now. Hefting the Henry, he moved to the first tent and pushed on the flap. He reckoned to find the inside a shambles but except for a few cups and silverware on the ground by a table, everything was neat and tidy.

Next was a cabin. Fargo poked his head in and let his eyes adjust before he entered. A table was set as if for supper, with plates and forks and spoons, and with a pitcher in the middle, barely a third full. He sniffed and dipped a finger in and licked the tip. Rosemary tea, unless he was mistaken, gone bitter from sitting there so long.

A half-knit shawl lay on a rocking chair. A candle on the mantle had burned down to a stub. The bed was fully made, with not so much as a ruffle in the quilt.

Fargo went back out.

Bear River Tom was just emerging from a tent, and he gave a little shudder. "When I said this is spooky, I wasn't kidding."

"You've seen worse," Fargo said, thinking of the aftermath of an Apache massacre they came upon a couple of years ago.

"Blood and ripped guts I can handle," Bear River Tom said. "Forty or fifty folks up and vanishing makes my skin crawl."

"We'll find out where they got to," Fargo predicted.

"What if we don't? What if something came along and took them?"

"Something?" Fargo said.

Bear River Tom shrugged. "A parson told me once that demons walk the earth."

"Demons, my ass."

"You don't reckon there are things in this world we can't see or hear but they're there anyway?"

"I never would have took you for a—" Fargo began, and stopped.

Up the gulch, a man screamed.

14

Troopers burst out of cabins and tents as Lieutenant Wright pointed and hollered, "That way! That way!"

Fargo broke into a run.

The scream rose to a piercing shriek, quavering with terror and pain, then ended in a ghastly throaty bubbling.

"Jesus!" Bear River Tom exclaimed, puffing to keep up. "Whoever that was is a goner."

Fargo thought so, too. He knew a death rattle when he heard one and that had sounded like a man in his final throes. He raced past the last of the tents. Ahead was a bend, the streamside thick with junipers.

"Be careful," Bear River Tom said, slowing. "We don't know what's around there."

Fargo aimed to find out. He raced around the turn and drew up short in consternation.

A figure was shambling toward him, a scarecrow in filthy clothes that hung in tatters. His hair was a matted mess, his face caked with dirt. His bloodshot eyes were wide in shock and his mouth worked but no sounds came out. He had his hands clamped to his throat but couldn't stem the scarlet spurting from between his fingers.

Bear River Tom dug in his heels and exclaimed, "Good God."

The man reached for them, his hand dripping blood. He took one more lurching step and then his legs buckled and he pitched onto his face.

Fargo was the first to reach him. Sinking to a knee, he set down the Henry and carefully rolled the man over. The care wasn't needed; the man was dead.

"Looks like someone slit his throat from ear to ear," Bear River Tom observed.

Fargo became aware of Lieutenant Wright and Private Davenport and the rest of the soldiers ringing them.

"My word," the lieutenant said in horror.

One of the troopers turned and took a few steps and retched.

"This ain't nothing, boy," Bear River Tom said. "Wait until you see what's left after the Sioux carve on a man."

"Do you suppose he was a settler?" Wright wondered.

Fargo went through the rags but found nothing. No poke, no papers, no clue at all to who the man had been.

Practically skin and bones, the palms of both his hands were thickly callused. Most puzzling of all, a sole on one of the man's shoes was missing and the man's foot was torn and bleeding.

"This poor bastard has been to hell and back," Bear River Tom remarked.

They followed his tracks all of six feet, to the stream. The man had waded out of it, apparently with his throat already slit.

Since they hadn't seen any sign of him downstream, he had to have come from upstream. Fargo and Tom paralleled it, seeking sign of where the man entered the water. After a quarter of a mile they stopped.

The sun was setting.

"We can't track in the dark," Fargo said, and bent his steps toward the settlement.

"What do you make of all this?" Bear River Tom asked.

"I'd like to know who killed that settler," Fargo said.

"You think he was one of them, then?"

"Who else would he be?"

"Where have the rest of them got to? What the hell were they doing here in the first place? Why did they walk off and leave everything? And what does that one-eyed devil who was shadowing us have to do with it? That's a heap of questions we need answered."

"You're forgetting one," Fargo said.

"Which is?"

"Where did their wagons and the teams and their other animals get to?"

Bear River Tom stopped in surprise, then kept walking. "Son of a bitch. I didn't even notice about the wagons. They've up and disappeared, too."

Fargo grunted.

"That's impossible. A wagon is heavy as hell. They leave tracks."

"Did you see any?"

"Only coming into the gulch. What happened to them after they were unloaded?" Tom scratched his chin. "I can't make hide nor hair of any of this."

The troopers had placed the body in a tent and covered it with a blanket. With Wright looking on, they were busy kindling a fire and preparing their supper.

"I take it you didn't find anything?" he said as they came up.

"I'll look again in the morning," Fargo said, and motioned. "What's this?"

"What does it look like? We have to eat."

"Out in the open where you can be picked off as easy as flies?"

"Where else do you suggest?"

Fargo motioned at the cabins and tents.

"I considered that," Lieutenant Wright said, "and put it to the men." He turned and raised his voice. "Private Davenport, front and center."

The general's son had just set down some firewood he'd gathered, and hurried over. "Sir?"

"Would you tell Mr. Fargo what the men told me when I suggested we sleep in the abandoned cabins?"

"We'd rather not," Davenport said, looking embarrassed. "This place has us jumping at our own shadows."

"You're safer inside than out," Fargo said.

"We know that," Davenport said, and lowered his voice. "Some of the men are afraid that whatever took the settlers will get them, too."

"The settlers were taken by surprise," Fargo said. The state of the camp clearly showed they were about to sit down to supper when calamity struck. "We won't be."

Davenport lowered his voice even more. "Some of the men say it couldn't have been Indians, like we first thought. That it has to be something else."

"You mean someone else," Bear River Tom corrected him.

"No, I mean some*thing*," Private Davenport said.

"Bullshit," Fargo said. He didn't believe in the supernatural. In all his travels he'd never encountered anything he couldn't explain. "We're sleeping in the cabins."

"We'd rather not," Davenport said.

"I wasn't asking," Fargo said. To Wright he said, "Pick three cabins. Assign three men each to two of them. You'll be in the third with Tom and me."

"He will?" Tom said.

Lieutenant Wright turned to Davenport. "You heard the man. Colonel Jennings says we're to do as he wants. So get cracking."

"I don't blame the soldier boys for being spooked," Bear River Tom said as the troopers hustled to obey. "I've never seen anything like this in all my born days."

"Don't forget Roanoke," Lieutenant Wright said.

"Who?" Tom asked.

"Not a who, a what. An early settlement in North Carolina."

"What about it?"

"Over one hundred men, women and children disappeared and were never found again."

"The hell you say," Tom said.

Lieutenant Wright surveyed the tents and cabins. "This could be Roanoke all over again."

15

Their cabin was the farthest into the gulch, with only a couple of tents deeper in.

Bear River Tom got a fire going and put coffee on to brew.

Fargo stood outside, the Henry cradled in his arms. To the north a wolf howled. To the south an owl hooted. And somewhere, the cry echoing and reechoing among the high peaks, a mountain lion screamed. He heard someone come out of the cabin and knew who it was without looking. "You'll need to keep a tight rein on your men."

"I know," Lieutenant Wright said. "They're young. It's to be expected."

Fargo refrained from pointing out that Wright wasn't much older.

"It's so dark without the moon," the lieutenant said. "I can barely see my hand when I hold out my arm."

"They call that 'night,'" Fargo said.

Lieutenant Wright chuckled. "So you do have a sense of humor."

"I get drunk enough, I'm hilarious as hell."

"I doubt that," Lieutenant Wright said. "You have a grim air about you."

"News to me."

"Your friend Tom says you're a natural-born hard case."

"Tom is full of shit sometimes," Fargo said, "especially when you get him started on tits."

"I resent that," Bear River Tom said, striding out to join them. "I'll have you know that I don't exaggerate more than the next gent."

"You once said that tits were God's gift to creation,"

Fargo reminded him. "If that's not being full of shit, I don't know what is."

Lieutenant Wright laughed.

"Just because you're more fond of legs than tits is no reason to speak ill of them."

"I'm not saying tits are full of shit," Fargo said. "I'm saying you are."

Wright laughed louder.

"Listen, you consarned nitpicker—" Bear River Tom began, and abruptly stopped.

From out of the depths of the gulch wafted a faint sound. It made Fargo think of a groan or a moan, only it rose and fell in ululating fashion, and ended with what sounded like a long-drawn-out sigh.

"What the hell?" Bear River Tom blurted.

Lieutenant Wright went pale and put his hand on the flap of his holster. "That didn't sound like an animal to me."

It didn't to Fargo, either. He led them past the last of the tents and cocked his head to listen but the moan or groan wasn't repeated.

"I've got more goose bumps than a goose," Bear River Tom whispered.

"What could it have been?" Lieutenant Wright asked.

"A man," Fargo replied. "Had to be."

"It wasn't entirely human," Wright said.

"Bullshit." Fargo was using that word a lot lately. "There's nothing else it could have been."

"I'm glad my men didn't hear it," Wright said, glancing at the other two cabins with lit windows farther off. "Some of them already think this place is haunted."

"A haunted gulch?" Fargo said. "How stupid are they?"

"Why not? There are haunted houses. I once heard of a haunted barn. And Private Benjamin tells me he lived near a haunted hill when he was growing up."

"Are you sure you went to West Point?"

"Scoff if you must," Wright said indignantly. "I'm only letting you know how some of the men feel."

"It's not as far-fetched as it sounds," Bear River Tom said.

"Not you too?" Fargo said.

"You know yourself that there are places the Indians won't go near. Bad medicine, they call them. Which is the same as saying they're haunted."

"I don't believe in ghosts," Fargo said.

"Who said it has to be the spirits of the dead?" Bear River Tom said. "It could be something else."

"Not that again. And I thought I knew you."

"You're too close minded, pard," Bear River Tom said. "You're as close minded about haunts as you are about tits."

"I don't want to hear any more haunt talk," Fargo told them. "It's silly even to bring it up."

"Could be you're right," Lieutenant Wright said. "But then, what's that?" And he pointed across the stream.

Fargo turned and felt his blood chill.

Above the far bank, something white was silhouetted against the night-shrouded pines and junipers. Vague and wavering, it was almost as wide as it was tall. As they looked on, the thing seemed to glide back into the trees and disappear.

"A ghost!" Bear River Tom exclaimed.

"Like hell." Fargo ran to the stream and waded out. The water came only as high as his shins. The gravel underfoot was slippery but he made it across without slipping and clambered up the bank.

Silence gripped the forest, a silence so complete as to be unnatural.

Fargo crept a few yards in, and hunkered. Loud splashing let him know the others had followed, and in moments they were crouched on either side, the lieutenant breathing much more heavily than the short exertion called for.

"Where did it get to?" he nervously whispered.

"How should I know?" Fargo said.

"It vanished," Bear River Tom said. "That's what haunts do."

"Enough of that nonsense," Fargo snapped. "Come morning we'll look for sign."

"And if we don't find any?" Tom said. "Will you be willing to admit you're wrong about spooks and such?"

"No," Fargo said. "I'll be pissed."

At dawn he was up and recrossed the stream before he had his first cup of coffee. He searched for half an hour but the carpet of pine needles was undisturbed.

"Well?" Bear River Tom asked when he opened the cabin door. "What was that white thing?"

"What it wasn't," Fargo said, "was a spook." He looked around. "Where's the lieutenant?"

"Soldier boy went to rouse the other boys in blue," Tom answered as he filled a cup with steaming coffee.

Fargo was all set to pour his own when the cabin door opened again.

"You need to come with me," Lieutenant Wright said anxiously. "You need to come right this second."

Fargo swore when he saw the troopers clustered at the horse string. Fearing for the Ovaro, he shoved through them and almost tripped over what they were staring at.

"We can't find a mark on it," Private Davenport said. "Not so much as a scratch."

A packhorse lay on its side, its eyes wide, as dead as anything. Its legs jutted straight, its tongue lolled. Flies were already gathering, and one crawled out of its mouth and took wing.

"It's still tied to the rope," a trooper said.

All the horses were in a string, a safeguard to prevent hostiles from stealing them. The smell of death had them skittish.

"Cut the others loose," Fargo commanded as he sank down next to the dead one. He roved his hands over its head, its neck, its back, its belly. Private Davenport was right—there wasn't a mark to be found.

"Maybe it's on the other side," Lieutenant Wright suggested. He ordered his men to roll the packhorse over.

After a lot of puffing and grunting, they succeeded.

Fargo bent to find the cause of death.

"Nothing," Bear River Tom said after they'd looked. "It's as if it keeled over for no reason."

"Could it have died of old age?" Lieutenant Wright asked. "Or was it sick?"

"No, and no," Fargo said. The sorrel was in its prime and as healthy as, well, a horse.

"Then what killed it?" another soldier said.

"I told you this place is haunted," a private by the name of Benjamin declared. "Now maybe all of you will believe me."

Fargo had never heard anything so ridiculous in his life. Then again, there was that white thing the night before, and now a packhorse dropped dead for no earthly reason.

What the hell was going on?

16

Fargo spent most of the day in the saddle. He roved a mile up the stream to near the end of the gulch but didn't go all the way.

Tracks were conspicuous by their absence. He found a lot of old ones in and around the settlement but not a single one past the first bend.

He scoured the opposite side and discovered deer tracks and coon tracks and possum tracks and the paw prints of a gray fox and two sets of coyote tracks. But nothing that would shed light on why the settlers vanished or explain the white thing or what killed the packhorse.

The sun was about to relinquish its rule when Fargo reined the weary Ovaro toward the settlement. He was as determined as ever to get to the bottom of the disappearances but it would have to wait for the new day.

The aroma of roasting venison made his stomach growl. Bear River Tom had shot a doe and her haunch was on a spit over a crackling fire.

"No need to tell me how it went, pard. I can tell by your face."

Fargo was in no mood for small talk. He nursed a cup of coffee and wished he had whiskey to add. No sooner did the desire cross his mind than Lieutenant Wright walked up and flourished a half-empty whiskey bottle.

"Look at what Private Davenport found."

Fargo snatched it and opened it and took a swig.

"Here now," Lieutenant Wright said. "You're not setting a good example for the men."

"That's your job," Fargo said, and wiped his mouth with his sleeve.

"I've had them start an inventory," Wright reported, "and what they haven't found is more revealing than what they have."

"Besides no bodies?" Bear River Tom said.

Wright paid him no mind. "They haven't found any money. No pokes, no purses, no bills, no coins."

"So much for your spooks," Fargo said.

"You saw a ghost with your own eyes and you refuse to admit it," Bear River Tom said.

"That thing last night was no ghost."

"When something looks like a duck and quacks like a duck it's a by-the-Almighty duck."

"Maybe it will come back tonight," Fargo hoped, "and we'll put it to the test."

"How do you test a ghost?" Lieutenant Wright asked.

"With lead," Fargo said, patting his Colt.

"You're going to shoot a spook?" Bear River Tom laughed. "When it doesn't drop dead, will you admit we're right?"

"No."

"God, you're stubborn," Tom said. "But now you have me hoping it comes back, too."

The troopers came and sat waiting for their evening meal. They were quiet and on edge and cast repeated glances into the gathering gloom of night.

Stars sparkled, and multiplied. A coyote gave voice to the yips of its breed. Not long after, up in the mountains, a bear roared.

Fargo was on his third cup of coffee when Tom announced it was time to eat. In addition to the venison, Tom had made biscuits. They were lumpy and twice the size a biscuit should be but they tasted right fine.

"You're not a bad cook," Lieutenant Wright commented, sounding surprised.

"When a man is on the trail as much as I am and has to fill his own belly," Bear River Tom said, "he learns a few tricks."

Fargo made the mistake of saying, "I'd like to know the trick of killing a horse without leaving a mark."

"That's easy," Private Davenport spoke up. "It died of fright."

Private Benjamin nodded. "From seeing that spook that's hanging around."

A third trooper threw in, "Even people can drop dead when they're scared enough. Their heart just stops."

"Enough of that kind of talk," Lieutenant Wright said sternly. "I'm not saying I believe this spook business and I'm not saying I don't. But we will conduct ourselves as soldiers whether there are ghosts or not."

"For the last goddamn time," Fargo said, "there are no such things."

As if to prove him wrong, the wind picked up and a moan filled the air, rising in volume and seeming to come from all directions at once. The same kind of moan as the night before.

Private Benjamin shot to his feet, exclaiming, "Do you hear that?"

Fargo had to admit it was unnerving. The short hairs on his neck prickled as he swiveled to try to pinpoint where it was coming from.

"Steady, men," Lieutenant Wright said. "Benjamin, sit back down and act your age."

Bear River Tom was frozen with a biscuit halfway to his mouth. "I ain't ever heard the like."

The moan ended as suddenly as it started, and in the silence that fell, Fargo could have heard a pebble drop.

"I vote we head back to Fort Laramie, sir," Private Benjamin said.

"When did this become a democracy?" Lieutenant Wright countered. "We've been given a mission by our commanding officer and we'll carry it out to the best of our ability."

"We can't fight ghosts, sir," a trooper said.

"I don't want to hear any more about it," Wright said. "That moan could just as well have come from a human throat."

For once Fargo and the young officer were in agreement. "Post a guard at the horses when we're done eating. We don't want a repeat of last night."

"Already done," Wright said.

"Pard?" Bear River Tom said, sounding strained.

"If it's ghosts or tits I don't want to hear it," Fargo said.

Tom pointed. "Then I won't say it's back."

Fargo turned and his neck prickled for a second time.

Across the stream in the pines, something white fluttered toward them.

17

Damned if Private Benjamin didn't scream.

Fargo dropped his cup and his plate and was up and running. He didn't think to grab the Henry but he had his Colt and that should be enough. Palming it, he reached the stream to find a deep pool blocked his way. He should go around but it would waste precious time. In he plunged, forcing against the water as it rose past his shins and his knees almost to his waist.

"Pard, wait!" Bear River Tom hollered.

Fargo wasn't about to. He could end the ghost nonsense once and for all.

The white thing had stopped and appeared to be hovering.

Fargo was almost halfway across, and fired. Nothing happened. The thing went on fluttering. He stopped and took aim and put two more slugs into the middle of whatever it was.

Just like that, the thing vanished. One moment it was there, the next it wasn't.

Moving as fast as he could, spraying water every which way, Fargo gained the other side. He was in the trees not thirty seconds after the thing vanished and it was nowhere to be seen. The only sounds were his heavy breathing and the pounding of boots and moccasins as the troopers and Bear River Tom hurried to reach him.

Fargo went farther in. The thing had to be there somewhere.

"Pard? Pard?" Bear River Tom, for all his bulk, was fleeter than the soldiers half his age. He reached Fargo's side and breathlessly scanned the woods. "What was it? Where did it get to?"

"I wish to hell I knew," Fargo growled.

"You hit it, didn't you?"

"Dead center."

"You know what that means, don't you?"

"Like hell it does."

Fargo roved in a circle that brought him back to the stream and the waiting troopers.

"You don't need to tell me if you found anything," Lieutenant Wright said.

"I saw it, sir, and I don't believe what I saw," Private Davenport said.

"What's the matter with all of you?" Private Benjamin said. "It's a spook of some kind. It has to be."

"I told you to stop with that kind of talk," Lieutenant Wright snapped.

"You saw it, sir," Benjamin persisted. "Did it look like a man to you? No. There was nothing human about it. It's a spook, I tell you. Some kind of thing from the other side."

"You try my patience, Private," Lieutenant Wright said. "Honest to God you do."

Fargo might have stood there longer, probing the woods, except he realized that they'd left their mounts and the remaining pack animal untended. "We have to get back."

"Shouldn't we conduct a search?" Lieutenant Wright asked.

"The horses, damn it."

Wright gave a start and ordered his men to recross at the double.

To Fargo's relief, the Ovaro and the other animals were perfectly fine. The dead one had been dragged off far enough that it wouldn't bring scavengers into the settlement, and to spare them from the reek when it began to rot.

Back at the fire, Fargo refilled his tin cup and hunkered.

"Well, that was exciting," Bear River Tom said.

"I should post men on the other side of the stream," Lieutenant Wright proposed. "They can alert us if the thing returns."

"Or have their throats slit in the middle of the night like that man yesterday," Fargo said.

"Which reminds me," Lieutenant Wright said. "We're so caught up with this spook, we've forgotten why we're here."

"I haven't," Fargo said.

Wright gestured at the empty cabins and tents. "Where can they be? How can so many people disappear without a trace?"

"The spook got them," Private Benjamin said.

Lieutenant Wright put his hands on his hips and glared. "Enough. So help me, if you bring it up again, when we get back to the fort I'll bring you up on a charge of insubordination."

Fargo was pleased to see Wright show some backbone. But it didn't go over well with the other troopers.

"Anyone else want to disobey an order?" Wright addressed them. "I will have discipline, gentlemen. Whether you like it or not."

"You sound like my father, sir," Private Davenport remarked.

"I thank you for the compliment."

"It wasn't intended to be, sir," Private Davenport said.

"If you don't like taking orders," Lieutenant Wright said, "you picked a damn poor profession."

Their petty squabbling was getting to Fargo. He stood and carried his cup around the cabin to where he could see the wall of forest on the other side of the stream. He wasn't alone long.

"These pups have a lot to learn," Bear River Tom grumbled.

Fargo grunted and sipped.

"How about if I go with you tomorrow? I told you before, I'm not cut out to be a nursemaid."

"As fond as you are of tits?" Fargo joked.

"Go to hell. You probably won't believe it but I haven't thought about tits all day."

Fargo looked up at the sky and then at the settlement and at the ground at their feet.

"What?" Bear River Tom said.

"I'm waiting for the world to end."

"I do have days when I don't, you know."

"Who are you and what have you done with the real Bear River Tom?"

"Go to hell twice. I'm not so—" Tom stopped.

From the settlement behind them rose a piercing shriek of terror.

18

Private Benjamin stood with his fly open and his hand in his pants. His mouth was open, too, and he was shrieking at the top of his lungs. He might have gone on shrieking had Fargo not run up and smacked him across the face.

Lieutenant Wright and the others got there moments later, the lieutenant holding a burning brand over his head to cast light. "What in the world got into you?" he demanded.

Private Benjamin pointed and his mouth worked a couple of times before he gasped, "Don't you see it? I had to take a piss and I came over and there it was."

Fargo had already seen, and an icy shiver ran down his spine.

"It's not possible," Bear River Tom said.

They had buried the man with the slit throat in a shallow grave and covered the mound with rocks to keep the wild things from digging it up. But now the rocks had been scattered and the dirt strewn about, and where the body should be was an empty hole.

Lieutenant Wright knelt and reached in and stated the obvious. "The body's gone."

"Who could have done this, sir?" a trooper asked, ripe with fear.

"It was the spook," Private Benjamin said.

"How would you like another smack?" Fargo said. He shoved Benjamin aside and squatted next to Wright. He reached into the grave, too. The earth was cool and dank to his touch. "This was done in the past half hour or so." Otherwise, the dirt would be drier and warmer.

"While we were off chasing that white thing," Bear River Tom guessed.

"Have your men conduct a search," Fargo said. "Use torches."

The color had drained from Wright's face but he nodded and briskly issued commands.

"Why steal the body?" Bear River Tom wondered when they were alone.

"To scare us."

"It's working," Bear River Tom said. "I'm scared as hell."

"Think of tits," Fargo couldn't believe he heard himself saying. "That should calm you."

"If it can't, nothing will."

They joined in the search, both of them with brands. Fargo examined the ground around the grave but couldn't find drag marks. "Whoever took it carried him."

"Why aren't there tracks?"

That was a good question. The scattered earth from the mound showed their own tracks and those of the troopers clear as day, but no others.

Fargo moved toward the granite bluffs and raised his brand as high as he could, seeking the telltale dark mouth of a cave. He did it on a hunch that didn't pay off.

"You ask me," Bear River Tom said, "the colonel should have sent fifty bluebellies instead of this pack of infants."

"The Sioux, remember?"

"Even so. There's not enough of us to deal with something like this."

They were a solemn group when they reassembled at the campfire.

"Not a sign of the body anywhere," Lieutenant Wright reported.

"Of course there isn't," Private Benjamin whispered to the others but they all heard him. "It was the spook, I tell you."

"Go guard the horses," Lieutenant Wright said.

Fargo had a lot to ponder. He stayed up long after Tom and the soldiers had turned in.

The wind had died. The gulch was as quiet as a cemetery. Around them, the mountains were another matter. Predator and prey were caught up in the nocturnal dance of death. The cry of a doe told of a meat eater's success, a snarl of frustration that a bobcat had missed a kill.

It was pushing one o'clock when Fargo went into the cabin. Stretching out, he tried to sleep. His mind was racing so fast, it was a losing proposition. Toward morning fatigue did what he couldn't.

The new dawn came much too soon. Fargo was aware of being shaken, and of Bear River Tom chuckling.

"Up and at 'em, pard. It's not like you to let the sun rise before you do."

Fargo felt sluggish. He went to the stream, stripped off his shirt, and splashed cold water on his face and chest until he was shivering and awake.

A trooper by the name of Arvil was preparing breakfast. "We're having flapjacks," he announced as Fargo came up. "But it will take a while."

"We're in no hurry," Lieutenant Wright said.

Fargo was. The sooner he resumed his hunt, the sooner they would learn the fate of the missing settlers.

"Excuse me, sir," Private Davenport said, "but has anyone seen Private Benjamin?"

"He stood guard over the horses last night," Wright reminded him.

"But where is he now, sir?"

The horses weren't a stone's throw away. Several were dozing, the Ovaro among them. But there was no Benjamin.

"Don't tell me he deserted his post?" Lieutenant Wright said angrily. "He'll wind up in the stockade if he's not careful."

Fargo spiced a splash of color and beckoned to Tom. They went to the string and there in the dust between two of the horses lay Private Benjamin's hat. Fargo picked it up and held it where Wright could see it. "The stockade is the least of his worries."

A frantic search ensued. Every cabin, every tent. Along the stream, along the granite bluff.

"He's vanished, just like the settlers," Lieutenant Wright summed up the result when they regrouped at the fire.

Fargo saw fear on nearly every face. He didn't blame them. The empty grave, the killing of the horse and now Benjamin disappearing, was enough to scare anyone. That made him think of the white thing in the trees and the moans.

Put it all together and there was only one conclusion. Someone was trying to scare them off. But why? That, too, was pretty obvious. To keep them from finding out what happened to the settlers.

"I'll be heading out as soon as we're done breakfast," he told them.

"By your lonesome?" Bear River Tom said. "With all that's going on, you should take me along to watch your back."

Fargo would like that but he had a greater worry, namely, the young troopers. They were so rattled, they weren't thinking straight. "I want you to stay here."

Tom looked at the troopers, and sighed. "I should give up scouting and open a home for infants. Do you still have that bottle? I need a drink."

"What we need," Lieutenant Wright said, "is an answer to all these mysteries."

"We sure as hell do," Fargo agreed, and with more than a little luck, by the end of the day he would have it.

19

He'd already searched the far end of the gulch. He'd already searched the forest across the stream. Today he decided to try along the granite heights.

There was a lot of granite in the Black Hills. It broke through the surface in the form of cliffs and bluffs and spire-like protrusions that sometimes rose hundreds of feet into the air.

Fargo started at the mouth of the gulch and scoured the towering heights. He hoped to find a way up. Noon found him at the far end, without success.

Damn, it was frustrating, he reflected. He had a sense that he'd missed something. That if he put his mind to the problem, the answer would leap out at him. He tried but it didn't, which only frustrated him more.

The sun was directly overhead when he made for the stream to let the Ovaro drink. In a grassy glade at the water's edge he drew rein and swung down. He hadn't had much sleep, and God, he was tired. He yawned and stretched and sat with his back to a juniper to ponder his problem.

It took a while for the sound he was hearing to break through his concentration. It came and it went, a hissing like that he'd once heard when he was at the Pacific coast and watched breakers roll into shore. It came from upstream.

About the fifth or sixth time, Fargo raised his head and said, "What the hell?"

It bore investigating. Taking the reins, he led the Ovaro.

He'd assumed that the water flowed down from higher up and on out the gulch. But he hadn't gone twenty yards when he discovered he was mistaken.

The stream was like the Rogue River in Oregon Country and a few other waterways. It didn't carry runoff down from a mountaintop. It flowed up out of the ground.

A dark cavity opened in the earth before him.

Now and again the water splashed against partially submerged boulders and made that hissing sound.

On either side was flat granite. Wide enough, Fargo noted, for a horse and rider. Hell, it was wide enough for a wagon.

He peered into the hole but couldn't see much. It appeared to incline gradually down but there might be an abrupt drop-off.

No one in their right mind would go into a hole like that but Fargo had another of his hunches. He tied the Ovaro to a spruce and gathered kindling and enough broken limbs for a fire. He also found a short, stout piece that he set aside.

He hated to cut his blanket but he had nothing else to use. He wrapped the strips around one end of the stout piece and knotted them so they wouldn't slide off.

When he put his makeshift torch to the fire, it caught right away.

Fargo moved to the hole. He didn't have a lot of time. Ten minutes at the most, and his torch would go out. Quickly, he descended, holding it in front of him so if there was a drop-off, he wouldn't go over the edge.

It was eerie, what with darkness all around and the water lapping at his boots. He hadn't gone far when he realized the sides had opened out and he was about to enter a cavern or underground chamber. He went a little farther and the truth dawned. It wasn't a cavern. It was a tunnel, created by the rushing water back when a lot more of it issued out of the earth.

His torch flickered in a gust of air, and he debated going deeper.

A new sound gave him pause, a faint *chink-chink-chink*, like that of metal striking rock. Cocking his head, he tried to figure out what it was.

The torch flickered again, and this time not from any breeze. It was going out.

Reluctantly, Fargo retraced his steps. He wasn't quite to the surface when the last tiny finger of flame died in a puff of smoke, plunging him in pitch-black. A few more steps, though, and he was awash in daylight from above.

Once out of the hole, Fargo stood scratching his chin. He could make more torches but they might not be enough to see him through to the far end and he'd be left in total darkness.

Fargo looked up. Above the hole, a forested slope rose to more granite. It was a steep climb but he would like to see what was on the other side of the mountain.

He turned and walked to the Ovaro and was reaching for the saddle horn when he glimpsed movement out of the corner of his eye. He whirled, dropping his hand to his Colt, and thought he saw a two-legged form gliding away from him.

Fargo broke into a run. Whoever it was, they were heading up the gulch toward the settlement, and the troopers.

He moved as silently as an Apache. So did the man he was pursuing. He moved more swiftly than most, too, just to keep up.

Not until the last bend before the settlement did Fargo get a good look at who he was following, when his quarry stopped.

It was the small man with the eye patch and the scar, the same deadly Metis who had tried twice now to kill him.

Crouching, Fargo closed in. He was near enough to shoot but he wanted the man alive. Unexpectedly, the Metis began climbing a tree. Fargo flattened. He wondered what the man was up to and it hit him that if the man climbed high enough, he could see past the bend to the settlement.

Smiling grimly, Fargo crawled. The small man had blundered. What went up must come down, and he would be waiting.

The man's agility was amazing. He leaped from limb to high limb, his body tucked tight. At one point he hooked his knees and performed a half flip that brought him to the next branch.

Fargo had never seen the like. He couldn't do that, and most people considered him uncommonly fit.

The man was well up now. He stopped, placed a hand above his good eye to shield it from the glare of the sun, and stood like a rock for several minutes.

It gave Fargo plenty of time to reach a small thicket and secrete himself.

High above, the small man lowered his arm and said something in French. His speed descending was twice what it had been climbing.

To Fargo it seemed that one second the man was sixty feet above him and the next he dropped lithely to earth.

Fargo coiled to spring. He expected the Metis to turn toward the settlement, and the moment that happened, he'd pounce. But to his considerable consternation, the man turned toward the thicket.

"You can come out, *monsieur.*"

Fargo wasn't about to. He suspected that he had waltzed into an ambush, and he would be damned if he'd make it easy for them.

"I know you are there," the one-eyed man said. "Just as I know you have been following me."

And here Fargo had been so sure he'd gone unnoticed.

"If you do not come out I will be angry with you," the one-eyed man said, "and believe me when I say that the last thing you want is to make Jacques Grevy mad. Those who do always wind up dead."

20

To stay hidden served no purpose. And besides, there were no signs of any others.

Fargo stood, his hand on his Colt. "Do you blow kisses to yourself in every mirror you see?"

Jacques Grevy laughed. "You suggest I am not humble enough? But humility is for the weak, not the strong."

"Is that so?" Fargo was puzzled by how calm this Grevy was, given that he had his six-shooter and Grevy had only a knife.

"*Très certainement.* You have seen for yourself, have you not, that some men are sheep and some men are wolves? You and I, my friend, we are wolves."

"I have a few good pards," Fargo said, "and you're not one of them."

"Such rancor," Grevy said. "You should be flattered I treat you as an equal."

"What I am," Fargo said, "is pissed that you tried to kill me."

"And now you will try to kill me, *oui*?"

"First some answers," Fargo said. "Why did you try? What do you have to do with the settlers who have gone missing? What did you do with a soldier by the name of Benjamin? And was it you who killed our packhorse?"

"So many questions," Grevy said. "Let's see. In the order in which you asked, I tried to kill you because it is wise, as you Americans say, to nip something in the bud. The settlers? Wouldn't you like to know. As for the rest, think of it as a game we play with three peanut shells and a peanut. You put the peanut under one of the shells and move them around and have someone try to guess which shell it is under."

"That made no damn sense."

"It does if you are me."

Fargo flicked his wrist and the Colt was in his hand. "Drop your pigsticker."

"And if I do not, you will shoot me?"

"In the balls."

"That is harsh, *mon ami*."

"I'm not your damn friend. And it's no more harsh than some bastard trying to stab me in the back."

Their eyes locked.

"*Oui*, I believe you would," Grevy said. "Very well."

To Fargo's surprise, the small man smiled and raised his arms over his head.

"I submit."

Fargo remembered their fierce fight in the saloon and how tough this little man was. "What the hell are you up to?"

"You have caught me. Do with me as you will."

"Drop the knife," Fargo repeated. He figured that Grevy would pretend to, then either rush him or throw it at him. Instead, with precise slow care, using only two fingers, Grevy plucked the knife from its sheath and let it fall to the grass.

"There. Do you feel safer?"

Fargo bobbed his chin at the bend. "Walk ahead of me. Any tricks and I'll put one in your spine."

"There are tricks and there are tricks," Grevy said. "But here and now I will behave."

Fargo didn't know what to make of him. But he wanted Wright and especially the troopers to see him with their own eyes.

It was Bear River Tom who spotted them first and gave a holler that brought the soldiers on the run.

"What do we have here?" Lieutenant Wright said.

"The spook," Fargo replied.

The troopers exchanged glances and Private Davenport said, "He's behind all the goings-on?"

"Him and his friends," Fargo guessed.

Jacques Grevy gave a slight bow. "You are most astute, *monsieur*."

"You admit it?" Lieutenant Wright said. Stepping up, he

grabbed the front of the small man's shirt. "Where's Private Benjamin? What have your people done with him?"

"What people, sir?" Private Davenport asked.

It was Grevy who answered. "Your kind calls us breeds, boy. Or half-breeds. They always say it with a sneer to show they disapprove. If they could, they would do to us as they have done to so many of the Indians who sometimes sire us, and wipe us out."

"You don't look like no breed to me, mister," Private Arvil said.

"That is because I take more after my father than my mother, who was Cree. But I assure you my blood is as much red as white."

"Where's Private Benjamin?" Lieutenant Wright again demanded.

"Where he should be," Grevy said.

Wright poked him in the chest. "I'm warning you. You'll tell us, one way or another."

"Will you torture me, perhaps?" Grevy asked in amusement.

"I just might," Lieutenant Wright said.

Grevy shook his head and laughed. "We both know it is against the rules you live by. You can bluster but you can't do the deed."

"How about me?" Fargo asked. "Can I do the deed?"

A hint of concern creased Grevy's scarred face. "You, yes. You have a hardness in you. You are a killer, like me."

"I'm nothing like you," Fargo said.

"Permit me to disagree. And grant me the respect I grant you. Yes, you would torture me. But I very much doubt I would say more than you would."

Fargo believed him.

Wright asked, "Where do you want to keep him until we get to the bottom of this?"

"In a cabin, bound hand and foot," Fargo said.

Wright was studying Grevy. "You know, his friends out there might be willing to swap him for Private Benjamin."

"I am not so important, I am afraid," Grevy said.

"You better hope you are, for your sake," Lieutenant

Wright said. He ordered Davenport and Arvil to take the prisoner to a cabin and tie him.

"Send four of them," Fargo said.

"That many for one man? And a runt at that?"

"Wolverines are smaller than bears," Fargo said.

"*Oui*," Grevy said, and flattered himself by adding, "It is not the size but the fierceness, *vous comprenez*?"

"I don't speak French," Lieutenant Wright said, "and you don't look all that fierce to me." He turned to two of the troopers. "Private Thomas and Private Reese, go along and cover him while Davenport and Arvil bind him."

Jacques Grevy gave a little bow to Fargo. "We will see each other again, you and I. We have unfinished business."

"Don't trip over your swelled head," Fargo said.

Lieutenant Wright turned to follow them. "Congratulations on catching him."

"I'm not sure who caught who," Fargo said. "He's up to something."

Bear River Tom had been unusually quiet. Now he broke his silence by saying, "Tits."

"You think of them at the damnedest times," Fargo said.

"No," Tom said. "I've been standing here racking my noggin. That handle of his, Jacques Grevy. I've heard it before. It took me until now to recollect where."

"I bet it has something to do with Anton Laguerre."

"How did you guess? Someone told me once, I can't remember who, that Grevy is Anton Laguerre's right-hand man. They grew up together, I think."

"And Colonel Jennings said he'd heard a rumor that Laguerre is involved somehow. Grevy proves it."

"You know what else it proves, don't you, pard?"

Fargo nodded. "That this is going to get a hell of a lot worse before we're done."

21

It bothered Fargo, how easily he had caught the little man with the eye patch. He'd like to question him some more but first he had to go get the Ovaro.

He hadn't liked leaving it off in the forest. But he couldn't very well have stalked Grevy on horseback.

To get there that much quicker, he borrowed a cavalry mount. Lieutenant Wright didn't object. Even a green officer recognized how important their horses were.

Relief brought a grin when he saw the stallion was where he'd left it. He rode up and dismounted. He was about to unwrap the reins from the spruce when he realized two things simultaneously. First, the Ovaro was staring into the brush, not at him. Second, his Henry was missing from the saddle scabbard.

He started to turn and to drop his hand to his Colt but froze at the click of not one but several gun hammers.

"Smart man," a voice said, with an accent similar to that of Jacques Grevy.

"Prenez votre main de votre revolver," another man said, then switched to English. "Take your hand off your revolver."

Fargo raised his arms chest high.

There were three of them. They wore the same kind of clothes and hats as Jacques Grevy—the stamp of the Metis. One held the Henry and another a single-shot Sharps. The last had a British-made revolver that Fargo seldom saw south of the Canadian border.

They were grinning and confident and the one with the Henry said, "It is a great trick we have played on you, *non*?"

"Let me guess," Fargo said. "You're friends of Jacques Grevy."

"No one is a friend of that one unless it is Anton Laguerre," the man with the Sharps said, "but we are of the same band."

"And not one of you is a ghost."

"Eh?" the man said, then laughed. "Oh. *Oui.* That was another great trick."

"You Americans," said the man who hadn't spoken yet. "You are *très superstitieux.*"

"Superstitious," translated the one with the Henry.

"How many are there in this band of yours?" Fargo asked.

"Ah, ah," said the man with the Henry. "That will be our secret for a while yet."

"You are coming with us, *monsieur.*"

"Anton Laguerre will want to talk to you," said the one with the revolver. He came closer and held out his other hand. "I will take your *pistolet, s'il vous plaît.* Pull it very slowly and give it to me."

"Slow as molasses," Fargo said. He lowered his right hand and extended two fingers and carefully plucked the Colt by the grips. He just as carefully drew it out of his holster and started to hold it out.

"Très bon," said the man holding the revolver on him.

The other two had let the muzzles of the Henry and the Sharps lower a little.

Fargo wasn't about to let them take him to Laguerre.

From what he'd heard, it would be the same as letting himself be captured by Apaches. Laguerre was fond of torturing his enemies—and anyone else—for the sadistic pleasure of it.

So as the man with the revolver reached out to take the Colt, he exploded into motion.

With a lightning flip and a twitch of his thumb, Fargo had the Colt in his palm and the hammer back and fired into the man's gut. He sprang to one side as the other two jerked their rifles up and fanned a shot into the face of the man holding the Henry and in the next heartbeat fanned a shot into the head of the other one.

In the bat of an eye all three were down, two of them dead. The man who was gut-shot thrashed and cried out, his hands spread over his badly bleeding belly.

"You shot me!"

"Where are the settlers?" Fargo asked.

The man grit his teeth and hissed, spittle dribbling over his chin. "Go to hell."

"Where's your camp?"

"Go to hell again." The man was scarlet from his navel to below his waist.

"What is your bunch up to?"

Red in the face, his veins bulging, the man rose on his elbows. "I will never tell you this side of the grave. Kill me and be done with it."

"Why not?" Fargo said, and squeezed the trigger.

Squatting, he quickly reloaded. Where there were three there might be more, and he was concerned the shots would bring them on the run. But there were no outcries, no pounding of hooves or boots. He finished and shoved the Colt into his holster and picked up the Henry.

Satisfied the three were alone, he rose, shoved the Henry into the scabbard, and gigged the Ovaro. Not back to the settlement but in a wide circle. When he didn't find what he was looking for, he expanded his search.

A whinny drew him into a stand of firs, and to three horses. One had caught the Ovaro's scent, and the same one whinnied again.

Their tracks showed that they came from the east. He backtracked, and was soon climbing the mountain. Steep slopes and several deadfalls slowed him so that he didn't reach the crest until late in the afternoon. Barely an hour of sunlight was left when he stopped and rose in the stirrups.

Far below lay a winding valley. He could see only part of it. There was nothing to excite his interest and he was about to rein around when he spied wisps of smoke at the bottom of the mountain.

A glance at the sun told him he wouldn't be able to get down there and back before nightfall. Since he didn't care to bumble around in the dark, he reluctantly turned around, descended to the three horses, threw the three bodies over them, and with stars twinkling overhead and wolves howling in feral chorus, he bent the Ovaro's legs to the settlement.

It took longer in the dark. As he neared the first tent,

someone challenged him with, "Who goes there?" Before he could answer, Private Davenport came toward him with his rifle to his shoulder. "Oh. It's you."

"Next time don't show yourself," Fargo advised, "or you could be picked off."

Davenport was staring at the bodies. "My God. Are they dead?"

"They're taking naps," Fargo said.

"Ask a stupid question, I suppose," Davenport said sheepishly. "I take it they're friends of our prisoner?"

"They were." Fargo gazed down the gulch. "Has he been behaving himself?"

"He hasn't given us a bit of trouble. Bear River Tom says he thinks that Grevy is up to something."

"So," said Fargo, "do I."

22

Privates Thomas and Reese were on guard outside the cabin. Their eyebrows rose at the sight of the bodies but they didn't say a thing as Fargo dismounted, slid one of the bodies off the horse it was on, and dragged it into the cabin.

Jacques Grevy lay on his side. His arms were behind his back and his wrists and ankles were bound. He raised his head and idly looked over and his whole body went rigid.

"A friend of yours?" Fargo said. He let the body drop and went back out and dragged in another.

Grevy had sat up, his scarred features a mask of fury. "You son of a bitch."

"I'm not done." Fargo brought in the third and dumped it over the other two, then hooked a chair with his boot and straddled it. "I thought you might like some company."

A string of invective burst from Grevy, a mix of French and English.

"So they *are* pards of yours," Fargo said. "Good friends, I hope."

"I will kill you for this."

"You've already tried twice," Fargo said. "As a threat that's not much."

Grevy nodded at the corpses. "You brought them here to rub my nose in it, as you Americans say."

"I figured you might want to pay your last respects."

"When I said you were a hard man, I truly had no idea how hard."

"Care to give me their names?"

"I will not," Grevy said. "What difference can it make? The important thing is that there are twenty-three more just like them who will be as eager to make you pay for this as I am."

Inwardly, Fargo smiled. So there were twenty-three more, were there? What else could he learn?

"Does that twenty-three include Anton Laguerre? Or doesn't he do his own killing nowadays?"

"What do you know of Anton?" Grevy said. "He and I, we were raised together. He is like a brother. And I tell you that as surely as the sun rises and sets, he will have your heart for this. He will have you staked out and cut it from your chest and the last thing you see will be it beating in his hand."

"I've heard he likes to carve on folks," Fargo said. "Has he been yellow all his life?"

"What do you mean?"

"Only a yellow dog kills someone who is helpless."

"Not if it is done for amusement, as Anton does," Grevy said angrily. "He would just as soon kill you in a fight. If you don't believe me, challenge him."

"I just might," Fargo said. "But now you have me wondering how many of these settlers he's carved on."

"None," Grevy said. "Why would he, when he needs them to—" He stopped and glared. "You son of a bitch."

"That's me," Fargo said.

Grevy regarded the bodies. "You dragged them in here to make me mad so I would talk without thinking."

"Damn," Fargo said. "I was hoping you wouldn't catch on for a while."

To his surprise, Jacques Grevy laughed. "I am impressed. You have a brain between those ears."

"Who doesn't?"

Grevy uttered a bark of contempt. "*Oui*, everyone has a brain. But few use it. These settlers you are so concerned over, for instance. They were on their way to Oregon Country but Anton tricked them into coming here."

"Did he, now?" Fargo said.

"It was a simple matter. He told them there was plenty of water and timber, and they would be safe from hostiles—"

"In the Black Hills?" Fargo interrupted. They weren't as well known back East as the Rockies but he imagined a lot of folks had heard of them, and of whites massacred by the Sioux.

Jacques Grevy's mouth curled in a wry smile. "You know

they are the Black Hills and I know they are the Black Hills, but the people with the wagon train think they are part of the Wind River Range."

"That's hundreds of miles from here."

"How would they know? Most of them can hardly tell north from south or east from west. Their wagon master, who could, was unfortunately kicked in the head by a horse and died."

"Did the horse walk on two legs?"

Grevy grinned.

"Let me see if I savvy all this," Fargo said. "Laguerre intercepted a wagon train bound for Oregon. He killed the pilot and fed the settlers a pack of lies and brought them to the Black Hills."

"Excellent," Grevy said.

"The settlers built a few cabins and started their settlement."

"*Oui.*"

"And now they've disappeared."

Grevy laughed. "They do not seem to be here, do they?"

"What has Laguerre done with them?"

"That is for me to know, *monsieur*, and for you to die finding out."

"I know where to look."

"Do you, indeed? It will be you and these young ones against two dozen of us. How long do you think you will last?"

Fargo nudged a body with his toe. "Longer than these three did."

"Touché."

Just then the door was flung open and in strode Lieutenant Wright. He was so intent on Fargo that he nearly tripped over the bodies. "What on earth?"

Fargo thought his eyes would bulge from his head. "I brought company for supper."

"There are times," Wright said, "when you're almost as bad as that tit-crazy Tom." He squatted and examined the corpses. "All three have been shot."

"I would have stomped them to death but they wouldn't hold still."

"See what I mean? At times you don't make any sense," Lieutenant Wright complained as he stood. "What do you want us to do with them?"

"Feed them to the coyotes and buzzards or bury them. It's up to you."

"It wouldn't be humane to let the scavengers have them. I'll form a burial detail." Wright wheeled on a heel and walked stiffly out.

"So young," Grevy said.

Fargo grunted.

"You would be wise to take them back to Fort Laramie and forget you were ever here. If not, they will surely die."

"I have a better idea," Fargo said.

"I am listening."

"I find Laguerre, I kill him, I kill you, I kill your friends, and we escort any settlers who are still alive back to the fort."

"You are one. We are many. How can you hope to prevail?"

Fargo nodded at the bodies. "Ask them."

23

"Thank the Almighty you're bringing me along," Bear River Tom said as the first glow of daylight lit the Black Hills.

Fargo was tightening his cinch. "I might need help and you're the only one worth a damn."

"Amen to that, brother."

"Did you get religion all of a sudden?" Fargo asked as he let down the stirrup.

"I need to get away for a while. These blue pups are so green they made grass look brown."

"That almost makes sense." Fargo gripped the saddle horn and swung up.

The settlement lay still in the chill dawn air. Two guards were outside the cabin that held Jacques Grevy. The rest were just rousing from sleep.

Lieutenant Wright emerged. "Brrrrr," he said, hugging himself. "I can't believe how cold it is this time of the year."

"It's the gulch," Fargo said. "It doesn't get enough heat during the day."

"Even so," Wright said, stamping a foot. "You'd think we were up in the Rocky Mountains."

"Try not to freeze to death," Bear River Tom said.

"And you try not to get yourselves killed," Wright replied. "If Grevy told the truth, we're severely outnumbered."

"We'll be back by nightfall," Fargo hoped.

"If you're not, I may and I may not follow your suggestion," Lieutenant Wright said.

"It was an order," Fargo said gruffly.

"Even so, I don't like to tuck tail and run. And that's what your order amounts to."

"What order?" Bear River Tom asked.

"To take Grevy back to the fort and have Colonel Jennings send more troops," Fargo explained.

"You should listen to him, pup," Bear River Tom said to Wright. "He's lasted out here a lot longer than you will."

Wright scowled. "I'm aware that neither of you think highly of my abilities but I'm more than competent to deal with this situation."

"Don't get cocky," Fargo said, and reined the Ovaro up the gulch.

"What he said," Bear River Tom said. "And a pair of tits, besides." He reined around and brought his horse alongside. "Life sure is peculiar, pard. We learn by experience but out here the experience can kill you before you learn."

"Know-it-alls think they don't need experience," Fargo said.

Tom chuckled. "So tell me more about this plan of yours."

"We find Laguerre."

Bear River Tom waited, and when Fargo didn't go on, he said, "That's it?"

"So far."

"I'll say one thing. You keep your plans simple."

"His men will be searching for the ones I killed."

"So we keep our eyes skinned or we lose ours."

On that grim note they brought their mounts to a trot.

Fargo rode easy in the saddle. He was so accustomed to the rhythm of the Ovaro that it was as if the two of them were one.

Bear River Tom spared him any mention of his favorite subject until they were halfway up the mountain and Tom's horse slipped and nearly fell. "Tits in a basket. This is a climb and a half."

"I've been meaning to ask," Fargo heard himself say before he could stop himself, "were you telling the truth about your ma?"

"And her three tits?"

"No, her three ears."

Tom chuckled. "It was sucking on them that made me the man I am today."

"Thank God she didn't have four."

They didn't utter another word until they reached the ridge that overlooked the valley. Tom broke their silence by pointing and saying, "Smoke."

84

"The same spot where I saw some yesterday," Fargo mentioned, more convinced than ever that he'd found Laguerre's camp.

"What if he's killed them all?" Bear River Tom asked.

"I doubt it," Fargo said. "Why lure them here just to slaughter them?"

"This is Anton Laguerre we're talking about. They say he carries a poke made from a gal he skinned."

"People say a lot of things."

"They say you're female crazy," Tom said, "and you sure as hell are."

"Says the gent who's never met a tit he didn't drool over."

"That's not true. I have my standards. I like them young and firm, not sagging and wrinkled."

"That's your last about tits for today."

"It is?"

"It is."

"You're getting as bossy as that colonel," Tom said, but he shut up and they headed down.

Fargo rode with his hand on his Colt. The slopes weren't as steep and there were few deadfalls. Two-thirds of the way down he heard a sound that brought him to a stop. Cocking his head, he listened.

"What is that?" Bear River Tom wondered.

It was the same *chink-chink-chink* that Fargo had heard in the hole at the end of the gulch. "My guess would be a pick."

"Why would they be chipping at rock?"

"Let's find out."

They commenced a slow stalk, staying on their horses until they heard voices and then dismounting and tying the reins and advancing on foot.

Fargo jacked a cartridge into the Henry's chamber, moving the lever slowly so it made less noise.

A rise blocked their view of what lay beyond.

Fargo dropped to his belly and crawled, the Henry against his side so it wouldn't flash in the sun and give him away. They reached the top and they both took off their hats and poked their heads up.

"I'll be damned," Bear River Tom said.

24

The encampment spread over ten acres or more. Nearly thirty wagons and carts were parked randomly about, their teams unhitched. The wagons weren't the heavy schooners preferred by emigrants. They were smaller and narrower.

Half a dozen cook fires were tended by women in full-length skirts and baggy blouses, many with scarves over their hair. Other women were doing wash in tubs or talking and lounging. Children played and scampered and laughed.

Large piles of firewood were near each fire. Something about them struck Fargo as peculiar.

"Anton Laguerre's band," Bear River Tom guessed. "But where are the menfolk?"

Fargo didn't see any, either. Ducking, he jammed his hat on his head. "Follow me."

It took a while to work their way to a bend in the near end of the valley.

"I'll be double-damned," Bear River Tom said.

There was another hole in the ground. Only this one was ten times as big as the one Fargo discovered on the other side of the mountain. A ribbon of water flowed into it, runoff from on high. Four men with rifles stood guard.

In the hole lights flickered and danced. Torches, Fargo figured. From out of it came the *chink-chink* sounds he'd been hearing.

"What the hell is going on in there, pard?"

"We need to sneak on down for a look-see."

Fargo was about to when several men came out of the hole. In the lead was a man who towered head and shoulders over the rest. He was so big and so broad, he dwarfed them.

"Anton Laguerre!" Tom whispered. "I've heard he's a he-bear."

So had Fargo.

"God, look at him."

Fargo was looking. He saw how the guards snapped straight and backed up as Laguerre approached. The men with Laguerre walked well back, as if wary of getting too close.

He remembered another story, how Anton Laguerre wasn't in his right mind, and he wondered if that was true, as well.

"I wish we were closer," Bear River Tom said. "I'd try to pick him off."

"Not yet," Fargo said. They had to find the settlers first.

Tom looked up at the mountains that ringed the valley. "I can understand why the Lakotas haven't found them yet. This place is pretty well hid."

Fargo was eager to see what lay down that hole. To try in broad daylight was out of the question. He'd be spotted before he got anywhere near it.

"What do we do now?" Tom asked.

"We wait."

The afternoon crawled like a snail. Nothing much happened.

Tom curled on his side and fell asleep.

Fatigue nipped at Fargo, too, but he stayed awake.

Twice Anton Laguerre returned to the hole. Each time he stayed down half an hour or so, and when he emerged, he carried a large leather sack that bulged and appeared heavy even for someone of his immense build.

The women and the children, Fargo noticed, never came anywhere near the hole. Once several young boys tossing a stick to a dog ventured close and were shushed away by the guards.

The sun was about to relinquish its reign when a bell clanged down in the hole and shortly thereafter out filed a bedraggled line of exhausted humanity.

Fargo had found the settlers.

Men, women, even children over the age of ten or so, plodded wearily toward the encampment. All were linked by rope around their ankles. Emaciated, filthy, haggard, they moved woodenly. Their faces were dull, any spark of hope long extinguished.

Nudging Bear River Tom, Fargo said, "You'd better take a gander."

Mumbling, Tom scratched himself and sat up. "Are they who I think they are?"

"Can there be any doubt?"

"They're being treated like animals. Some of them are on their last legs."

More guards with rifles had emerged and were prodding the line along.

Just then a bearded captive in badly torn clothes stumbled and fell to his hands and knees. It brought the line to a halt. He tried to rise but lacked the strength. Another man bent to help him but one of the guards snarled a command and stalked over.

The man on his hands and knees looked up just as the guard brought the butt of his rifle crashing down.

A woman screamed. A young girl wailed.

The settler lay in a spreading pool of crimson, his forehead staved in.

It took only a few moments for other guards to remove the rope from the dead man's ankle. Brusquely, cruelly, they goaded the others along.

"Well, now," Bear River Tom said. "Did that rile you as much as it riled me?"

The settlers were ushered into the open and allowed to collapse about twenty yards from the wagons.

Many of the Metis women and children stopped what they were doing to stare. They didn't seem to like what they saw.

Anton Laguerre appeared from out of a big tent. His angry bellow put an end to the staring.

"Some of those folks won't last out the week," Bear River Tom predicted. "What does that bastard have them doing?"

"As soon as the sun sets, I aim to find out."

"I'm going with you."

"Think again. One of us has to be able to ride for help in case something goes wrong."

"Well, damn."

Food smells wafted on the air. Fargo had been to Metis camps before, and the supper hour was a time for them to relax and talk and laugh. There was little of that here. They sat for the most part in glum silence. Now and then a glance strayed to the wretches bound by the rope.

Fargo began to wonder. The Metis were no different from any other folk. There were good ones and there were bad ones. There were ones who would share the shirt off their backs and ones who would stick a knife in your back for the poke in your pocket.

"Almost time, pard," Bear River Tom said.

A molten red sun was dipping below the mountain. It would not be long before it set.

Fargo handed the Henry over. "Hold on to this for me."

In the dark the Colt would suffice.

"Be careful, you hear?"

"Always," Fargo said. He started down the rise but Tom wasn't done.

"If they catch you and kill you, what do you want me to do?"

"Persuade Wright to head for the fort and tell Colonel Jennings he needs to bring half his command if he's to have any hope of saving these people."

"I'll do that, sure enough," Tom promised. "And one more thing, besides."

"I'm afraid to ask," Fargo said.

Bear River Tom grinned. "I'll squeeze a pair of tits in your memory."

25

Sticking to the darkening shadows, Fargo reached the bottom of the mountain unseen. He was about a hundred yards from the hole. The ground between was wide open.

The wagons, though, were far enough away that he doubted anyone would spot him. Just to be safe, he eased down and snaked through the grass.

The lights in the hole had gone out. He figured no one was there until he heard a cough.

Instantly, he froze.

A lucifer flared, bathing a bearded face. A man held it to the bowl of a pipe, and puffed.

Someone else said, "Laguerre catches you smoking, he'll kick your ribs in."

"He said not to light a lantern," the smoker said. "He didn't say anything about pipes. And why are we speaking English and not French?"

"Fewer know it."

"Ah. You worry we will be overheard."

Fargo inched forward.

The pair were partway in the hole, visible from the waist up.

"I must confess," said the man who wasn't smoking the pipe, "that I almost feel sorry for them."

"Almost?" said the other. "Did you see that little girl? Her ribs stick out."

"What can we do? Over half the men side with him and the others are like us. They don't dare object for fear for their families."

"Maybe once he has enough he will leave us," the man with the pipe said.

"You dream," said the other. "He likes having people under his thumb. He likes inflicting pain."

"He is an animal," the smoker said, and spat.

Fargo had no doubt who they were talking about. His face low to the ground, he inched near enough to see that they were seated on a rock shelf.

"Did you hear that Grevy hasn't returned?"

That got Fargo's attention.

"Good riddance. He is worse than Laguerre." The smoker blew a cloud of smoke.

"I have heard a rumor," the other man said, and raised his head to peer toward the encampment as if to assure himself he wouldn't be overheard. "They say Laguerre sent him and three others to scare off the soldiers. And if they can't be scared off, to slay them."

Fargo felt a spike of concern for Lieutenant Wright and the young troopers. But Grevy was bound and being watched. They should be all right until he returned.

"Laguerre goes too far," the smoker said. "He will bring the army down on our heads."

"I hope the rumor is true, then. We would be rid of him, and of her. Not even they can fight the United States Army."

By then Fargo was close enough that he had a decision to make. Should he kill them or take them down some other way? From the sound of things, they were part of a faction that opposed Anton Laguerre. He decided to gamble.

Palming his Colt, he slid to the edge and pointed it and thumbed back the hammer.

At the *click* both of them glanced up in alarm.

"Make a move," Fargo said quietly, "and you're dead men."

The smoker's mouth fell open and his pipe nearly slipped out.

The other one blurted, "Who are you? What do you do here?"

"I'm with that army you were just talking about," Fargo said. "And we're here to put a stop to Anton Laguerre."

"How many soldiers are with you?"

"Forty," Fargo lied. "They're waiting for my signal to attack. But first I want to know what's in this hole."

"You don't know?"

Fargo rose into a crouch. "Shed your hardware, gents. I don't need to tell you to pretend you're made of molasses, do I?"

They were anxious to please. When they had set their weapons down, they raised their arms and the man with the pipe said, "I am Claude. This is my friend, Pierre. We are of the Red River Metis," he ended proudly.

"You're a long way from home," Fargo said as he slipped into the hole and used his foot to slide their weapons farther away.

"We are not here because we want to be," Claude said.

"No, our leader has brought us," Pierre threw in.

"I heard you talking," Fargo revealed. "I take it you're not fond of Anton Laguerre?"

"We despise the pig," Claude said bitterly. "There is a rift among us, American. Where before we were all as one, and happy with our lives, now many dislike our leader and the acts he makes us do."

"How many dislike him?" Fargo needed to know.

"Perhaps ten of the men. The rest do his bidding without question."

Pierre spat in contempt. "Laguerre is a brute. He is not content to hunt and trade. Since he took control, he kills, he steals, he rapes. And the fools among us go along with him."

"Why don't you do something about it?"

"We have our families to think of," Claude said.

Pierre nodded. "In the early days several men stood up to him. They, and their loved ones, are no longer with us."

"Will you help us?" Fargo asked. "We don't want to hurt your people if we don't have to."

"Forty soldiers, you say?" Claude said. "Not even Laguerre will dare to defy that many."

"What would you have us do?" Pierre asked.

"Spread word to those you can trust," Fargo said. "Tell them to be ready to rise up when we attack."

"We will do that, gladly," Claude said.

"Good." Fargo intended to bring Wright and the troopers back, and with some of the Metis to aid them, put a stop to the brutal state of affairs. "Before I go, I want to see in this hole."

"Come. We will show you," Claude offered. He picked up

an unlit lantern and proceeded to light it, adjusting the wick so the glow didn't spread more than a few feet. He raised it shoulder-high and started down, Pierre falling into step beside him.

Fargo followed, his Colt leveled. He trusted them only so far. "Explain the digging."

"It is not digging, it is chipping," Claude said.

"And panning," Pierre added, gesturing at the stream.

"As for an explanation, it is simple," Claude said. "The Black Hills are rich in gold."

26

The ground sloped and the hole widened. A tunnel stretched before them, with a dirt wall on one side and a rock wall on the other. And there, in the rock, were yellow streaks, some as wide as Fargo's arm. Veins of gold ore.

Fargo whistled.

"This goes on under the mountain and comes out the other side." Claude confirmed what Fargo already knew.

"But the gold is only at this end," Pierre said.

They went farther.

Fargo saw picks and shovels and pans that lay where the captives had dropped them when their forced labor was done for the day. "So this is why he lured them here."

"You have figured that out, have you?" Claude said. "*Oui*. Laguerre, or, rather, his *femme*, his woman, persuaded them that here was better than Oregon. That they would have plenty of water and graze for their livestock, and best of all, they were safe from unfriendly Indians."

Fargo had heard all that already, except for the part about Laguerre's woman. An important piece of the puzzle was missing, though. "How did Laguerre know there was gold here?"

"We Metis, we have traded with many of the tribes for a great many years now," Claude said. "Since before the days when beaver were trapped for their plews. We trade with tribes who would never trade with you whites."

"The Lakotas, for instance," Pierre took up the account. "They hate your kind. They resent that you spread across the land like locusts, and they fear that you will try to take their land as you have taken the land of the Creeks and many others."

94

Claude nodded. "But they do not hate or fear us. We are, after all, of mixed blood. And while they do not accept us as equals, they do not look down their noses at us, as you Americans would say, and do."

Now Pierre nodded. "It was a Miniconjou who told Laguerre about the gold. An old warrior who in his youth rode all over these Black Hills and knows them better than perhaps any man alive."

"Laguerre traded with him and the old man invited Laguerre into his lodge to eat and drink," Claude related. "Laguerre saw that the old warrior's wife wore a necklace made of what the warrior called yellow rocks. Laguerre knew them for what they were."

Pierre did more nodding. "Laguerre got the old man drunk and the old man told him about this place. About the hole and the stream."

"It changed Laguerre," Claude said. "He became worse than he was, a thing I did not think possible. Before he learned of the gold, he was mean and brutal and a bully. After he learned of the gold, he became a *homme obsédé*, a man obsessed."

"And as crafty as ever," Pierre said. "He knew it would take a lot of work to get the gold out of the ground. And he is not fond of work. Not that kind. Nor, I must admit, are many of the others."

Fargo savvied, and swore. "He lured the settlers here to do his digging and panning for him?"

"Oui," Claude said.

"And now you know all there is to know," Pierre told him. "As much as we do."

Fargo had heard enough. It was time he got out of there. "I'm obliged. I'll tell the soldiers everything you've told me."

"They must act soon," Claude said. "Not just for the sake of our poor prisoners."

"There are the Sioux to worry about," Pierre said.

Fargo was puzzled. "I thought you Metis are friends with them."

"How shall I put this?" Claude said. "Yes, they trade with us. We give them guns and knives and things they cannot get anywhere else. But that is as far as our friendship goes.

They allow us to enter their country, and to barter, and once that is over, we must leave their land."

"They will not like that we are here," Pierre said. "They will not like that we do this."

"That's why Laguerre is working the settlers to death," Fargo said. "He wants to get in and out as quickly as he can."

"With as much gold as he can," Pierre said.

"He defeats his own purpose, though," Claude said. "He works them too hard. Already five have died and many others are ready to drop."

"He doesn't give them enough food or let them rest enough," Pierre said. "It is pitiable."

"And your people do nothing to help them?"

"Some of our women take them food. And we look after their youngest children."

Claude removed his pipe from his mouth. "We worry what Laguerre will want done with them once he has enough gold."

"How do you mean?" Fargo asked.

"Laguerre's woman has mentioned several times that it is best if there are no witnesses. Not even the young ones."

"He wouldn't," Fargo said.

"Do not put anything past Anton Laguerre," Claude said.

"Or his woman," Pierre said.

"You've mentioned her a few times," Fargo noted. "What's she like?"

"She is a serpent, that one," Pierre said. "A perfect mate for a perfect beast."

Fargo had learned more than enough. "Let's go," he said, motioning for them to precede him.

They were almost out of the hole when Claude said over his shoulder, "You give us hope, American. For that we are grateful."

"*Oui,*" Pierre said. "Those of us who hate Laguerre have prayed for this nightmare to end."

"Is that a fact?" a gruff voice said, and suddenly they were bathed in light.

Fargo coiled and looked up—into the muzzles of half a dozen rifles.

27

"Drop that pistol or I will have you shot to pieces," the gruff voice demanded.

Fargo squinted against the glare. At least three lanterns were blazing, maybe a fourth. He knew that if he so much as twitched wrong, the rifles pointed at him would blast him to ribbons. "Hold your fire," he said, and with great reluctance, he set his Colt on the ground.

Claude and Pierre seemed to be in shock.

"Anton!" the latter exclaimed, recovering first. "This man jumped us and disarmed us."

"I can see that," growled a great bulk that hove into view. "How unfortunate for you but fortunate for me." He laughed a cold laugh. "So you have prayed for this nightmare to end, have you?"

Pierre took a step back and thrust both his palms at the bulk. "I said that for his benefit, to trick him. To make him think he could trust me."

"Can I trust you?" Anton Laguerre growled.

Pierre had broken out in a sweat. "I give you my word, Anton. Haven't I stood by you from the start? From when you challenged old Victor for leadership and won?"

"Yes, you have. But I have never thought you were sincere."

"How can you say such a thing? You have no more faithful a supporter than me."

"If that is true, it's a shame I must kill you," Laguerre said, and a new muzzle appeared, trained on Pierre. "Any last words?"

"*Non!*" Pierre cried.

"That's all? No tender message for your wife? Or for your children?"

"Please, Anton."

"Do not worry about them," Laguerre said. "I will force her to take another man and he will look after them for you." He laughed at that.

"You can't," Pierre pleaded.

"I have never liked that word. When someone says I can't, I always want to show them I can to prove them wrong."

"Please."

The revolver muzzle exploded with flame and lead. Pierre's head jerked to the impact of the slug, which caught him in the center of his forehead, drilled clean through, and burst out the rear of his head. Without uttering a sound, Pierre folded in on himself and was still.

"Mère de Dieu," Claude gasped.

"As for you," Laguerre said. "Do you feel as he did?"

"Never," Claude anxiously replied. "I am as loyal as anyone."

"Then why did you tell this American that he gives you hope?" Laguerre said. "I heard you with my own ears."

"Oh, God."

"Now you see? That is part of your problem right there. You pray to that which doesn't exist. There is no God, Claude. Surely you have learned that by now. All the people you've seen slain. The baby that one time, when the cabin burned down?"

"Accidents happen," Claude said. "You can't blame those on the Almighty."

"I don't. I just finished telling you God doesn't exist. We are on our own. I will show you. Pray to your God that I don't shoot you and we'll see if He stops me."

"I beg of you."

"Let me hear you pray, Claude."

Fargo was helpless to act with so many rifles still trained on him. He tried, though, by saying, "You can't blame them. I took them by surprise."

"I will get to you in a minute, American," Anton Laguerre said. "Be patient." He paused. "I am waiting, Claude."

Claude prayed. He dropped to his knees and raised his

clasped hands to the heavens and cried, *"Seigneur du ciel et de la terre, aidez-moi!"*

Half a minute went by and no one spoke or moved and Laguerre's massive silhouette bent. "Nothing, Claude. It is as I said. Make peace with yourself."

Claude swung his clasped hands toward Laguerre. "I pray to you, then, Anton."

"Quoi?"

"If God will not answer me, I pray to you. Spare me, for the sake of my loved ones."

Anton Laguerre did the last thing Fargo expected—he threw back his head and roared with mirth. "You pray to *me*? Am I your new god, then, Claude?"

"If you want to be, yes."

Laguerre laughed harder. "Oh, this is wonderful. You amuse me, Claude. For that, and that alone, you have earned a second chance."

"Thank you." Claude burst into tears and lowered his forehead to the earth. "Thank you, thank you, thank you."

"Don't make a spectacle of yourself." Laguerre came along the rim and stood over Fargo. "Now we come to you, American. To who you are and why you are here."

"I won't tell you a damn thing," Fargo vowed.

"You misunderstand. You do not need to. I already know much, thanks to Jacques. He described you to me. You are the scout, the one he tried to stop from bringing the soldiers."

Fargo stayed silent.

"I sent him to the fort to learn if your army was aware of the missing settlers. He heard the colonel order the lieutenant to bring you to his office."

Despite himself Fargo said, "And tried to knife me in the back in the saloon."

"Oui. He followed you when you guided the soldiers here and tried to shoot you but again you were lucky."

"He came close," Fargo admitted.

"It is unlike Jacques to fail to kill a man once, let alone twice. I have been very curious about you. Very curious indeed."

Since Laguerre was being so talkative, Fargo prompted

him with, "Why the hell did he kill that horse and dig up the body and flap that sheet in the trees?"

"Grevy overheard some of the young soldiers say that they thought the settlement was haunted. She and I thought that if we could scare them off, it would gain us the time we need to get out more gold."

"She?" Fargo said, although he knew who Laguerre was talking about.

"*Ma femme.* My wife. I make no decisions without her. I would have as soon killed all of you but she convinced me that would bring your army down on us and we did not want that."

"So she has all the brains?" Fargo said.

Anton Laguerre didn't reply right away. When he finally did, he said, "You insult me. It shows you have spirit. And you will need all you have for what I have in store for you."

"I hear you're fond of staking folks out and skinning them alive."

Laguerre sighed. "Do something once and you never hear the end of it. No, *Monsieur* Fargo. I never do it the same way twice. I like to be—what is the word?—*creatif.*"

"You know my name?"

"Do you not listen? I just told you I know all about you. But enough. You will come out of the hole with your hands in the air or the six men pointing rifles at you will shoot you in the balls."

"You call that creative?"

Laguerre laughed. "You have a sense of humor, too." He beckoned. "We must become better acquainted before you die."

28

The moment he climbed out, Fargo was seized, his arms were roughly jerked behind him and his wrists were bound. He saw there were others besides the six with rifles, about a dozen, all told.

The bulk that was Anton Laguerre poked a thick finger at Claude. "Since Pierre and you were such good friends, I leave it to you to bury him. Remember the lesson you have learned this night or the next time we bury you."

The men with the lanterns moved back a little, and Fargo finally had a good look at the infamous Anton Laguerre.

Up close, the Metis' size was even more impressive. The width of his shoulders was remarkable. He had the body of a bull, a body most men would envy, but the same couldn't be said of his face. It was as craggy as the granite heights of the Black Hills, with bulging cheeks and a hooked nose, and deep lines. One eye was brown and the other was blue. The brown eye had a tic. It constantly moved back and forth and up and down. When Laguerre blinked, only the blue eye closed. The eyelid to the brown eye stayed open.

Fargo couldn't help himself. He stared.

"Ah. You admire my beauty mark, yes?" Laguerre said, and laughed. He touched the afflicted eye. "I have had this since I was a boy. I was kicked by a pony and this was the result."

The men with the rifles and lanterns formed a ring around them and Laguerre motioned him toward the camp.

One of the men poked Fargo in the back with his rifle to be sure he took the hint.

"Are the little boys in blue up there watching us?" Laguerre asked.

"I came alone," Fargo said. "We caught your friend Grevy. They're watching him."

"They think they have caught him," Laguerre said, and chuckled.

Fargo didn't like the sound of that. "You're not what I expected."

"How so? I'm uglier? Handsomer? Bigger? Not as dumb as you imagined?"

"Bringing those settlers here wasn't very smart," Fargo said.

"*Au contraire.* We could not do the panning and digging ourselves and keep watch for the Lakotas at the same time. So they do the work for us."

They neared the spot where the emigrants were under guard. Several fires had been kindled and the captives were huddled around them, scarecrows craving warmth.

"They won't last much longer, the shape they're in," Fargo said.

"They will have served their purpose and that is the important thing." Laguerre stared at them with ill-concealed contempt. "I feed them enough to keep them going. They do not need more than that."

"There are women and kids."

"So? The more that work, the faster it goes."

Pale, unhealthy faces, the eyes dull and listless, fixed in fear on their captor as he passed.

"Sheep," Laguerre said, and spat. "It makes me sick to look at them."

Fargo noticed a girl who wasn't much over ten, her arms and legs as thin as sticks, her face sunken with exhaustion and hunger. Right then and there he made up his mind that before this was over, he'd do his damnedest to kill all those who were to blame.

"I see by your face that you pity them, American," Laguerre said. "Save your pity for those who deserve it."

They came to the tents and the wagons and carts. In a normal Metis camp everyone would be talking and smiling but here an air of tension hung over them, as if they were waiting for the keen edge of an ax to fall.

"Not a happy bunch, are they?" Fargo said.

"They must be as quiet as they can in order not to alert the Sioux."

"Or could it be a lot of them don't like what you're up to."

"You should not believe everything Pierre and Claude might have told you. My people are devoted to me."

"They look it."

Fargo was ushered to the largest tent in the encampment. The flaps had been tied back and inside were chairs and a table and even a rug. "Your palace?"

"No. Mine," a woman said, and from around the side appeared a vision.

She stood well over six feet and was as finely shaped as any female since Eve. Her hair was red with brown streaks, which she wore loose in a long mane. Instead of a dress she wore men's clothes: a shirt, pants and boots. A wide leather belt with a revolver on one hip and a knife on the other somehow seemed to fit her. She planted herself in front of Fargo and looked him up and down. "The scout," she said, a statement, not a question.

"Oui," Laguerre said. "We caught him at the diggings."

"I heard a shot."

"Pierre spoke ill of me," Laguerre said.

The woman's green eyes flashed. "You couldn't have whipped him? There will be grumblings."

"I can handle the malcontents."

"I hope so, for both our sakes." She turned back to Fargo. "But where are my manners. I'm Marie Laguerre. It is a pleasure to meet you."

"I can't say the same."

"Why not? I am very fond of men. Especially handsome ones like you."

Anton Laguerre scowled, deepening the lines in his craggy face. "Don't start."

"I play with him," Marie said. She smiled and touched her husband's cheek. "You are the only one for me. You know that."

"I know I do not like when you play with others."

"Supper is about ready," Marie changed the subject. "Bring him in and we will eat." She went back around the side of the tent toward a cook fire.

Fargo was prodded to the table and forced to sit in a chair. To his mild surprise, the rope was removed from his wrists. But in case he got ideas, two men with rifles stood well back, covering him.

Anton Laguerre sat at the head of the table. He ran his huge hand over the top and said, "My woman likes her luxuries."

"You haul all this around for her?" Fargo said. "It must be true love."

"Again you taunt me. But, yes, it is. I care for Marie as I have cared for no other. We are very much alike, she and I."

"Does she skin people too?"

"She has, in fact," Laguerre said. "She is not a sweet buttercup, that one. She will kill you as quick as look at you if you give her cause."

Something for Fargo to remember.

"You haven't noticed yet, have you?" Laguerre said, and pointed at a corner.

Fargo shifted in his chair.

Bulging packs and pouches were piled knee-high over a five-foot area.

"The gold," Fargo said.

"What else? As you can see, enough for Marie and I to live like kings the rest of our lives."

"What about the rest of your people?"

"They will all get a share."

Something in the way the giant said it told Fargo they sure as Hades wouldn't.

Marie came back in and took a seat. She sat straight and proud, a queen at court, her green eyes lingering on Fargo. "Are you comfortable? Your last meal should be pleasant."

"Is that what this is?" Fargo said. "Why go to the bother?"

"You would rather we kill you outright?" Marie grinned and shook her head. "We have so little to entertain us. And I hate being bored."

"As do I," Laguerre said. "Enjoy this while it lasts, American. For tomorrow you will scream in pain and beg me to kill you."

29

Fargo had never met a pair quite like the Laguerres. Both were coldhearted killers who gave no more thought to snuffing a human life than they would to swatting a fly. Both seemed to think it was their natural right to lord it over their people, and woe to anyone who dared to disagree.

Several girls entered, carrying food. Not one was over ten. At first Fargo took them for Metis. Then he saw how apprehensive they were, and the grime on their faces, and how their dresses needed washing, and he turned to Marie and said, "You bitch."

Anton Laguerre heaved out of his chair and bunched his huge fists.

"*Non,*" Marie said, holding up a hand. "Sit back down. He is mad about *les filles*, is all."

"They're settlers' daughters," Fargo said.

"*Oui.* I have them wait on me hand and foot, as the expression goes. In return I feed them and don't have their parents killed. Isn't that kind of me?" Marie laughed, then sobered and glared at Anton. "I told you to sit back down."

Like a puppy chastised by its master, Laguerre obeyed.

A girl came around the table and carefully set a plate in front of Fargo. He smiled and she quickly bowed her head and looked away, but not before he saw bruises on her face and neck. His throat constricted and his blood boiled, and he said, "Well, now."

"Pardon?" Marie said.

"The condemned isn't hungry," Fargo said. In truth, he was famished, but he'd be damned if he'd show them he was.

"Come now, *monsieur,*" Marie chided. "The girls have worked so hard. Would you insult them by not eating?"

Fargo barely stopped himself from lunging out of his chair and slamming his fist into her face. As calmly as he could, he asked, "How often do you beat them?"

Her fork poised over her plate, Marie said, "Eh? Oh, I hit them when they don't behave. But that is what any parent does, is it not so?"

"Do you have kids of your own?"

Marie looked at Anton and frowned. "*Non*. We have tried but one of us is not able to pass on his seed."

"Hell, woman," Laguerre growled. "Tell him all our secrets, why don't you?"

"Don't be mad, *mon cher*. I have long since resigned myself to it."

Fargo couldn't stand to look at her. He never knew that Laguerre had a wife. Never would have suspected that she was more of a monster than her husband.

"You should at least try to eat," Marie said.

Fargo picked up his fork and knife. He wasn't going to, but the slab of roast buffalo meat and buttered potatoes made his mouth water. And he did need to keep up his strength.

"That's better," Marie said when he took his first bite. She waved a hand at the girls. "Out you go. I will call you if we need you."

Laguerre stabbed at his food with his fork, the *chink* of metal on the plate loud.

"What is the matter with you?" Marie asked. "Why are you mad?"

"You know damn well why."

"Don't take that tone with me. I can no more not be true to my nature than you can't be true to yours."

"Fancy words," Laguerre said. "You always have an excuse."

"I have needs."

Fargo wondered what in hell they were talking about.

"Don't talk to me of needs, wife," Laguerre said. "Do I do what you do?"

"You know better."

Laguerre set down his fork so hard, it was a wonder his

plate didn't break. "You are the only person alive who can talk to me like that."

"And you are the only man who gets to spend entire nights with me, so we are even."

Laguerre snorted. "I should be grateful for your great gift, is that it?" He suddenly stood. "I have lost my appetite. I will be back later." With that, he beckoned to the two men covering Fargo and all three walked out.

"I do so despise it when he acts like that," Marie said.

Fargo marveled that they'd left him unguarded.

Marie must have guessed what he was thinking because she said, "Do not get any ideas. I will not hesitate to shoot you if you try to escape. And if you look out the tent, you will see that those two didn't go far."

The pair with the rifles had, in fact, taken up positions on either side of the flaps.

"It's just you and me now," Marie said, and smiled seductively.

"Oh, hell," Fargo said.

"You seem taken aback."

Fargo was. "You rub his nose in it and he still lets you?"

"*Lets* me?" Marie said. "No one tells me what I can and cannot do. Not even him."

"Either you're dumb as hell or you must be something special."

Marie rimmed her red lips with the tip of her tongue. "Can you guess which?"

"Damn, lady."

"Have no fear. He won't come storming in and gut you with his knife."

"So you say."

"Let me make it plain," Marie Laguerre said. "I have Anton wrapped around my little finger. Anything I want, I have only to ask. It has been this way since we met. He is, as you might say, smitten."

"Was it you who came up with the idea to come here for the gold?"

"Who would not desire to be wealthy?" Marie rejoined. "Yes, I put him up to coming here. And, yes, it was my idea to use the settlers. I am, as the British would say, the power behind the throne."

"You're something," Fargo said.

"I get what I want," Marie declared fiercely. "And at the moment, I want you."

30

Fargo shook his head in amazement. "Damn me if you're not serious."

"Why would I not be? Let's finish our meal. The condemned man, as you call yourself, will need to be at his best later. Disappoint me and you will die that much sooner."

Fargo forked a piece of potato. Since she was being so talkative, he decided to fish for information. "Where does Jacques Grevy fit into your scheme of things?"

"Grevy?" Marie said. "He has been Anton's friend since they were boys. He is strange, that one. He cares neither for women nor gold. He has only one passion in life."

"What would that be?" Fargo asked when she didn't go on.

"Killing."

"Not much of a passion."

Marie laughed without warmth. "No, it is not. He makes a sport of it. To test himself, he says. Once he let himself be captured by some white trappers who had issues with us just to see if he could escape from them."

"That's loco," Fargo said. But he was thinking of how easily he'd caught Grevy himself, and how smug the man had been about it.

"I agree. He takes needless risks. I would rather be in control of a situation than throw myself into peril to see if I can survive as he is doing with those soldiers you are with."

"You don't say."

"When Anton failed to scare them off, we decided it would be best to wipe them out."

"And bring the army down on your heads?"

"It will be a while before the colonel at Fort Laramie

sends more men to find out what happened to them. By then we will have as much gold as we need and will be well on our way to Canada."

"You have it all thought out."

"It is what I do best. And another reason Anton will never harm a hair on my head. He is a great leader of men but he is not a great thinker. That is where I come in."

Fargo had to get to the settlement and warn Wright. But that would take some doing.

"You think a lot, yourself," Marie remarked.

"It's a bad habit I can't shake."

She placed her elbows on the table and thrust her bosom out. "So tell me. Would the condemned man care for a last taste of the fruit of the forbidden tree?"

"Is that what they call it in Canada?"

Laughing, Marie said, "I am being discreet. I am, after all, a lady."

No, Fargo almost said, you're anything but. "How about if you blow out the lanterns and we get to it?"

"Not so fast," Marie replied. "It is early yet. We will wait until most of the camp is asleep. I have Anton to think of. We can't have everyone whispering behind his back."

"How considerate of you."

Her cheeks colored and she said, "Insult me again and I will have you tied and beaten and in the morning Anton will put an end to you."

"It wasn't an insult," Fargo added to his lies. "You can't be the power behind the throne if there's no throne."

That seemed to mollify her. "Very true. You have no idea. But as you can see, it's worth the effort. I live the best of all our band. And if they presume to complain, Anton deals with them."

"I never heard of a Metis band like this one."

"There isn't any. We are unique. Rogues, you might say. The other bands think we give them a bad name." She laughed merrily.

"You sure have opened my eyes."

"It is too bad they will be closed permanently before the new day is out."

On that note she fell silent and concentrated on her meal.

Fargo ate without tasting much. He was working out how to escape. Slipping from the encampment wouldn't be easy, what with the guards and the dogs, but if he could reach the forest he was confident they'd never catch him.

After a while Marie clapped her hands several times and the little girls returned to bear the plates away.

"Would you care for dessert?" she asked.

Fargo smiled and looked at her breasts. "Those will do me just fine."

"Oh my," Marie said, pleased. "Come midnight or so, you will have your wish. But now, if you will excuse me, there are people I must talk to."

Fargo watched her walk out. She did have a nice ass.

It was a shame she was about the most vile human being he'd ever come across.

He looked around for a weapon but if there was one, it was well hidden.

A shadow filled the tent, and without looking up he said, "That's some woman you've got there."

"She is everything to me," Anton Laguerre said.

"Yet you let her play with other men."

"Don't rub my nose in it," Laguerre warned. "That wouldn't be wise."

Fargo met his cold gaze. "They have a word for men like you. Two words, actually. One of them is whipped."

Laguerre bristled. His huge hands opened and closed and he took a step but stopped. "No. It would make her mad."

"Whipped as whipped can be."

"For that, American, I will make an example of you. You will suffer as no one has suffered since the dawn of time."

"Sticks and stones," Fargo said.

"You remind me of Jacques. He, too, is always so calm in the face of danger. He, too, is always secretly laughing at others. But you will be laughing out your ass when I am done with you." Laguerre turned to go.

"One thing," Fargo said.

"Eh?"

"Does she like to be on top or the bottom?"

It was a wonder steam didn't come out of Anton Laguerre's

ears. "You provoke me. Why?" He cocked his head. "You are up to something. What is it?"

Fargo hadn't figured on him being so shrewd. "It's as you said. I like to provoke folks. It comes naturally."

Laguerre grinned a death's head grin. "Dying will come naturally, too."

31

Fargo was left alone in the big tent. He got up and prowled about and then saw the guards peering in at him and sat back down.

Seldom had time dragged so slowly. He hated that he had to wait to make his break. For all he knew, Jacques Grevy was making a break of his own.

Outside, the camp grew quiet. The few voices stilled. There was less moving about. Some of the lanterns he could see out the front flaps were extinguished.

He wondered what was keeping Marie. He wondered if Bear River Tom would become impatient and come down to see what was going on. He wondered if Lieutenant Wright and Private Davenport and the rest were still alive.

Suddenly Marie was there. She said something to the guards, then entered and closed the front flaps and tied them. "So we will not be disturbed," she said over her shoulder.

"We wouldn't want that," Fargo said. He sure as hell wouldn't.

Marie turned and pointed at the bearskin rug. "Make yourself comfortable."

"Why not?" Pushing his chair back, Fargo rose and moved to the rug and sat with his knees bent and his arms draped over them.

Unbuckling her gun belt, Marie moved to the table. She set her revolver and knife down and came over to stand above him with an odd sort of smile on her red lips and her hands on her hips. "You are about the handsomest man I've ever laid eyes on."

"I know what I'd like to lay," Fargo said.

"That is not how this works," Marie said. Without warning,

she flicked her right foot out, slamming her boot against his chest and pressing him flat onto his back.

"What the hell?" Fargo said, grabbing her ankle.

"Ah, ah," Marie said, shaking her head and wagging a finger. "I'm in control. I'm always in control. You don't make love to me. *I* make love to *you*. Think of me as the man and you as the woman."

Fargo resisted an urge to wrench on her leg and upend her. "This will be different."

"I don't care for your tone. Don't tell me you're one of those who can't stand it when a woman is in the saddle?"

"Ride away," Fargo said. He would play along for a while to get her off her guard.

"First things first." Marie removed her foot and went to a small chest. Kneeling, she opened it. Her back was to him and he couldn't see what she was taking out. When she stood and turned, she had handcuffs in one hand and a riding crop in the other.

"What the hell?"

"My toys," Marie said. "I have a lot more." She nodded at the chest. "Before we're through, you'll see every one."

Fargo sat up. He wasn't about to let her cuff him. She might not free him again. "You never said anything about this part."

"Why should I? You will do exactly as I say and as I want or we will end this now and the guards will take you away." Marie came to the rug and wagged the cuffs. "Take off your shirt and put your hands behind your back."

Fargo glanced at the flaps. Were the guards listening? he wondered. Were they even out there? He removed his hat and set it aside.

"We don't need that," Marie said, and kicked it.

The hat flipped end over end and landed a few feet away.

Fargo frowned. "You shouldn't have done that."

"When will you get it through your head? You don't tell me what to do. I tell you. Now get that shirt off."

"Yes, ma'am," Fargo said. He pulled and tugged the buckskin up over his shoulders and head and placed it next to him.

Marie kicked that, too.

114

Fargo stared up at her and smiled. "This is going to be fun."

"Now you're getting into the spirit of things." She stepped behind him and set down the riding crop. "Your wrists, if you please. And even if you don't."

Fargo kept on smiling and looked over his shoulder. "Here you go," he said, and shifted his arms behind him. She reached for his left wrist and opened a cuff to snap it on. Whirling, he seized her forearm and shoved her onto the rug. Before she could stop him, he slid his knee between her thighs and cupped her breast while swooping his mouth to hers.

For a few moments Marie was completely still. Then she exploded. She dropped the handcuffs and pushed at his chest with both hands and pulled her head away, saying, "God-damn you. Get off me."

Fargo squeezed her tit, hard.

"I mean it!" Marie hissed, and tried to ram her leg into his groin.

Rolling onto his side, Fargo propped his head in his hand. "Something the matter?"

Marie swore. "You don't listen. I told you. *I* am in control. *I* say how we will make love. Not you."

Fargo eased onto his back and placed his hands behind his head. "Get making, then. Just be careful of that bulge in my pants."

Marie looked down. A hunger came into her eyes, and they widened. "You are hard already?"

"A tit will do that," Fargo said, and was glad Bear River Tom wasn't there.

"You and a stallion have something in common."

"Why don't you find out just how big I am?" Fargo sought to distract her from the handcuffs.

She was reaching for them, but stopped. "Will you lie there and behave?"

"As God is my witness."

Cupping his crotch, Marie ran her hand the length of his pole. "Oh my. You know, I have never understood how big men can have small ones and small men can have big ones."

"For a woman who says she wants to make love, you sure do gab a lot."

"All these muscles," Marie said, placing her other hand on his washboard gut.

"Gab, gab, gab."

"I will show you," Marie said. Eagerly, she worked at loosening his pants, and yanked. He had to raise his backside in order for her to pull them low enough.

Sitting back, she undid her blouse and left it on but open. She removed her boots and slid her pants off. Under other circumstances he would have been amused to discover she had on nothing underneath.

"God, I want you," Marie said huskily. Rising, she straddled him, gripped his member, and slowly impaled herself.

Fargo did nothing to help. She wanted control, she could have it so long as she didn't go for the cuffs.

Throwing back her head, Marie closed her eyes and gasped, "Ohhhh. You feel good."

So did she but Fargo stayed quiet.

Placing her hands on his chest, Marie moved her hips in a languid pumping motion. "I should warn you. I like to take my time."

"You know what they say," Fargo said.

She arched an eyebrow.

"The longer, the better."

"In more ways than one," Marie said, and laughed. "Now let's get to it."

32

Some would say that Fargo had bedded more than his share of females. But never, ever, had he ever been with a woman like Marie Laguerre. When he reached for a tit, she slapped his hand away. When he raised his head to try to kiss her, she shoved him back down. She wasn't fooling when she said she wanted to be in control.

So long as the cuffs stayed out of it, Fargo didn't mind. He had time to kill, anyway.

Closing her eyes, Marie ran her hands over his chest and neck. She bent and bit his ear so hard, it hurt. Then she bent lower and sank her teeth so deep into his shoulder, she drew drops of blood.

Wincing from the pain, Fargo said, "Didn't you have enough supper?"

"You are a big baby. So what if I like a little blood with my lovemaking." Marie grinned and licked the drops while looking him in the eyes.

Weirdest damn woman ever, Fargo thought. But again, so long as she didn't bite him where it counted most, he'd play along.

Marie arched her back and closed her eyes. She went on slowly rocking her hips for a good long while. Now and then she'd shudder and pucker her lips and utter little gasps.

Fargo lay there and let her have her fun. At one point he forgot himself and covered a hard nipple with his palm, only to have her open her eyes and glare and angrily slap his wrist away.

"No, damn it."

"Bitch," Fargo said.

To his amusement, Marie smiled. "Yes," she said huskily. "Talk dirty to me. I like it when they talk dirty."

"I like it when I'm not treated like a lump of meat."

"But handsome," Marie said, her smile widening, "that's all you are."

Soon after that she gave another of her little gasps, and sat still, her chin bowed.

"Are you falling asleep?" Fargo joked. For him, this was about the most boring lovemaking ever. He might as well be doing it himself.

"And you say I gab?" Marie retorted. She looked down and licked her lips. "Now we get to the good part."

"I actually get to touch you?"

"You whine too much." Marie twisted and reached for the riding crop.

"You don't want to do that."

"Relax. Pain with pleasure heightens the pleasure." She hefted the crop and raised herself off his pole. "My, oh my. Still hard. You are amazing."

Fargo glanced at the front flaps. A lot depended on whether the guards were still there. Somehow he doubted she'd let them listen. He hoped he was right.

"Roll over," Marie commanded.

"If I don't?"

"I will give a yell and this tent will fill with men who will beat you and bind you, and then I will give you to my husband."

Fargo did as she wanted. Her legs were on either side of him, and when he looked up, he could see between hers. He couldn't recollect the sight of a woman's private parts ever exciting him less.

"By the time I am done," Marie boasted, "you will beg me to stop."

"Just remember this was your notion," Fargo said.

"Of course it was mine," Marie said. "I always do as I want, not as others want. I have been this way since I was a small girl."

"You don't say."

"I think you belittle me," Marie said. "I do not like being treated with contempt."

Fargo had a thought. "Is this how you make love to Anton?"

"But of course. He is so big and so strong, but he is mine to bend to my will. You should see him. So docile, so tame. Sometimes he curls into a ball and whimpers."

"I'll be damned."

"All men are like that, deep down."

"Not all."

"You are wrong. And I will show you how wrong you are." Marie slapped the riding crop against her palm. "Prepare to bleed."

"If you say so." Fargo had his head slightly turned and was watching her out of the corner of his eye. He saw her raise the crop, saw the wild gleam that came into her eyes, a lust that had nothing to do with pleasure and everything to do with pain.

"This is the part I like best," Marie informed him, and slashed the riding crop down.

Fargo twisted and lunged. He blocked the riding crop with his left forearm even as he drove his right fist into her gut. He didn't hold back. He punched her full force and it doubled her over. She gurgled and opened her mouth to shout and he hit her on the jaw. Not once but three times, just as hard as he could.

Marie folded.

Catching her, Fargo set her on the bearskin rug, crouched, and listened. There were no outcries from out front. He quickly hitched up his pants. He hated to let a good hard-on go to waste but she repulsed him. He donned his shirt and his hat and strapped on his gun belt.

The last he'd seen of his Colt, Anton Laguerre had him set it on the ground at the diggings. He helped himself to Marie's Smith & Wesson, checked that it was loaded, and shoved it into his holster.

Marie groaned.

Sliding her arms behind her back, he used her own handcuffs on her wrists. He drew the toothpick and cut a strip from her shirt, wadded it, and stuffed it into her mouth. He had to work fast. She was reviving sooner than he expected. He cut another strip and tied it across her mouth, then helped himself to her belt and secured it around her ankles. As he rose and stood back, she opened her eyes.

"Have a nice nap?"

Hatred contorted her features. She tried to speak and realized she was gagged, then attempted to kick him with both feet.

Sidestepping, Fargo drove his boot into her belly. She cried out, the sound muffled by the gag, and bent in half, snot dribbling from her nose.

"You must love the pain," Fargo said.

When she stopped quaking, she glared. And if looks could kill, he'd be dead on the spot.

"I should slit your damn throat," Fargo said. But Anton might take it out on the captives and he couldn't have that.

She said something. He didn't need to hear the words to know she was cursing him.

"I love you, too," Fargo said, and winked.

Working swiftly, he rolled her up in the bearskin rug. She struggled but there wasn't much she could do. When he was done, he crept to the front flaps.

Outside, the camp was quiet and still.

As silently as possible, Fargo opened the flaps just enough to peek out.

The guards weren't there.

Fargo smiled. Turning, he ran to the rear of the tent. A slash of the toothpick, and he slipped into the night.

From here on out, it was do or die.

33

The encampment was dark. All the campfires save one were out. The fire still crackling was over near the captives. Several men sat around it, and judging by his size, Anton Laguerre was with them.

Staying low to the ground, Fargo made for the forest. He had acres to cover, acres of tents and carts and wagons and sleeping, snoring forms.

Then there were the dogs. They worried him more than anything. All it would take was for a cur to set to barking and the whole camp would leap to arms.

Twice he had to flatten. The first time was when a man stirred and sat up and gazed sleepily about and then lay back down. The second time, a dog came around a cart and saw him.

Fargo froze. He braced for a snarl or a yip but all the dog did was sniff a few times and go back around the cart.

When, at last, the forest closed around him, Fargo rose and circled to the pit. He heard noises before it came into sight.

Claude was burying Pierre about twenty feet from the opening. A lit lantern, the wick so low it hardly cast a glow, was at his feet. Every now and then he muttered in French. His back was to the hole.

Dropping flat, Fargo crawled. It might be too much to expect but he crawled down in and groped around, and to his delight, found his Colt. He set the Smith & Wesson where the Colt had been and was halfway out when he sensed someone behind him. Whirling, he extended the Colt but he didn't shoot.

Claude stood on the other side, leaning on the shovel.

"You," he said simply.

"You saw me? Why didn't you holler for the others?"

Claude glared at the glowing campfire a hundred yards away. "Why should I? You saw what that pig did to Pierre. You saw how he treated me. He made me beg. Made me grovel for my life."

"Your people would be better off if he was dead," Fargo planted a seed.

"Do you think many of us don't know that? Him and her, both. They are animals. They are worse savages than the red men your kind hate so much."

"Tell me something," Fargo said, careful to keep his voice down. "If I come back with the troopers, will we have to fight all of you? Or just the ones who side with him and that bitch?"

Claude sniffed. "I, for one, would not lift a finger to help either. But if the soldiers attack, most would see it as an attack upon us all, and resist."

"Not if you spread word that we're only after Anton and Marie."

"Would that I could."

"Why not? Less blood would be spilled. Fewer people would die."

"*Oui.* But I don't know who I can trust. Oh, there are some, like me, who have made no secret of the fact they are not happy. A lot of others share our hatred but they wisely keep their feelings to themselves." Claude gestured at the grave he was digging, and the body. "You can understand why, yes?"

"Damn," Fargo said.

"I am sorry. Were I to tell the wrong person, they would go to Anton and he would not spare me a second time. Not only that, he and his wife would be forewarned of your coming."

"It was worth a try." Fargo turned to go.

"American?"

Fargo stopped.

"They are the key. Kill them and their followers will be like a snake without a head."

Again Fargo went to go but Claude wasn't done.

"Something else. When we first heard that soldiers had

come, Marie gave orders that if we are attacked, her men are to kill the settlers."

"What?"

"Out of spite. She has a black heart, that one."

"I'm obliged," Fargo said.

Claude shrugged. "I hate them, American. I hate them more than I have ever hated anything my entire life. The day they die, I will celebrate."

Fargo got out of there. It was a long climb to where he'd left Bear River Tom, and he had time to think. He considered telling Wright to send to the fort for more troopers but that would take days and there was no predicting what Marie and Anton would do to the captives in the meantime.

The smart thing was to do exactly as Claude suggested.

Cut off the head of a snake and the snake died. In this instance there were two heads but the one was more a footstool.

A boulder loomed in his path and he went to go around it when a figure blocked his way.

"Took you long enough, pard!" Bear River Tom exclaimed. Grinning, he clapped Fargo on the shoulder. "I took you for a goner."

"Thanks for lending a hand."

"Hey, now," Tom said, sounding offended. "I saw them take you but there wasn't anything I could do."

"Nice of you to stick around."

"That's hardly fair," Tom said. "I reckoned to wait until an hour or so before dawn when even their dogs would be asleep, and sneak on in to rescue you." He paused. "What happened down there? How did you get away?"

"I'll tell you all about it on the way to the settlement."

They rode as fast as the darkness and the terrain allowed. It wasn't much before dawn when Fargo drew rein at the last bend.

"Why have we stopped?" Bear River Tom asked.

"We go on foot from here," Fargo said, dismounting.

"How come, if I'm not being too nosy?"

"Grevy," Fargo said.

"They had him trussed up and under guard. What could he do?"

"A man like him, a lot." Fargo yanked the Henry from the saddle scabbard and cat-footed toward the first of the tents. He might be going to a lot of trouble for nothing but he remembered Anton Laguerre saying that Grevy had let himself be caught. Why, unless it was to kill the troopers the first chance he got? And what better opportunity than after Tom and he left?

"Look yonder," Bear River Tom whispered, and pointed.

Awash in starlight, a uniform-clad form lay in front of a cabin, its arms outflung.

"Cover me," Fargo said, and glided over. The body was facedown but he knew who it was before he rolled it over.

Private Arvil had been knifed between the shoulder blades. The whites of his eyes showed in the shock he felt as the cold steel penetrated his flesh.

Fargo straightened and beckoned to Tom.

The next body lay half in brush. They would have missed it if not for a boot that jutted out. Private Reese's throat was a gash from ear to ear.

"We never should have left these infants alone," Tom said bitterly.

They crept on.

The front door to the next cabin was open and a rectangle of light spilled from inside.

A shadow moved across it.

Instantly, Fargo hunkered. He motioned for Tom to stay put and stalked to the door. Taking a deep breath, he swung inside, ready to blast away.

34

Private Thomas was sprawled on the floor in a pool of dry blood. Above him, hanging from the main rafter with rope around their ankles, were Lieutenant Archibald Wright and Private Davenport. Both were tied at the wrist and gagged. As the sight of Fargo and Bear River Tom, they erupted into frantic motions, bobbing their heads and trying to make themselves understood through their gags.

Tom ran to Wright. "Hold still, damn you," he said. A sharp tug and he had the gag out.

"A trap!" the lieutenant bawled as Tom turned to do the same for Private Davenport. "It's a trap, for God's sake! He hung us here as bait!"

Fargo threw himself against the inside wall just as a rifle boomed.

Bear River Tom was sent stumbling as if by an invisible push. He caught himself, recovered, and staggered over to a table, clutching his left shoulder. "I'm hit, pard."

Darting to a lamp on a stand, Fargo blew it out, plunging the interior in gloom.

Out in the gulch, Jacques Grevy laughed. "Quick thinking, *monsieur*. But it will not help you. You are at my mercy."

Fargo sidled to the door and slammed it shut. Gloom filled the cabin but he could still see to get around.

"Cut me down," Lieutenant Wright requested. "Hurry."

Instead, Fargo moved to the table. "How bad?"

"I think he was going for a heart shot but I moved," Bear River Tom said, his hand propped on the table to keep him up. "I'm bleeding like a stuck pig."

"Cut me down, damn it," Wright said. "Cut both of us down."

Fargo went to the window. Frilly curtains covered it, courtesy of a feminine touch. He cautiously parted them and immediately a rifle banged and lead whipped at the left curtain and sizzled past his ear.

"Almost, eh?" Jacques Grevy shouted, and laughed.

Fargo swore. The bastard was playing with them.

"Why are you over there?" Lieutenant Wright angrily demanded. "Why haven't you cut us down yet?"

"Quiet," Fargo said. He was trying to listen for movement outside.

"We can help you. It'll be the four of us against him. He won't dare try to rush us."

"Shut up, damn you."

"I will not. I've been hanging here for hours. I can barely feel my legs and my head hurts and it's a wonder I'm still conscious."

"Pard?" Bear River Tom said.

Fargo moved through the darkness to the table. He merely had to touch Tom's shirt and his fingers became wet. "I need to tend this."

"I hate to be a bother."

"We'll need light," Fargo said. He'd have to relight the lamp.

"A candle would be better," Tom said. "I saw one over on the chest of drawers."

Fargo went to the corner where the chest sat. Tom was right. A candle would cast less light. There would be fewer shadows for Grevy to fire at.

"What about us?" Lieutenant Wright started in again. "Why aren't you listening to me? And where have you been, anyhow? We're the only two left. Our prisoner killed all the rest of my men. If you'd been here, maybe he wouldn't have. I blame you in part for their deaths, I'll have you know."

Fargo smothered a burst of anger. He saw the candle and grabbed it. "Tom, did you happen to see anything I can light this with?" His lucifers were in his saddlebags on the Ovaro.

Bear River Tom didn't answer.

"Tom?" Fargo said. Hurrying over, he put a hand to his friend's shoulder.

Tom jerked his head up and opened his eyes. "Sorry. I keep blanking in and out."

Private Davenport, who hadn't uttered a word so far, cleared his throat. "I can light it for you."

Fargo set down the candle, grabbed a chair, and dragged it over under the rafter. Drawing his toothpick, he stepped up. "Brace yourself in case it slips."

"Yes, sir."

"Cut me down first," Lieutenant Wright broke in. "We'll free him together."

By rising on his toes, Fargo got hold of the rope above Davenport's boots. Gripping it with his left hand, he commenced to slice with his right. He cut slowly, bracing himself. Suddenly the rope began to give. He clutched it with both hands just as it parted and Davenport dropped.

He almost toppled from the chair but held on, and there was a thump. "Are you all right?"

"I banged my head a little but I'll live," the young trooper replied.

Stepping down, Fargo cut him free.

"Thank you," Davenport said. "I need a minute. My hands are numb. Let me get the feeling back."

"Tell me about Grevy. How did he get loose?"

"I don't rightly know," Davenport said. "He killed all the others before he came after us. I was talking to the lieutenant and he jumped us and disarmed us and brought us in here. He had the lieutenant tie me and hoist me up and then he did the lieutenant."

"Who is still hanging here, damn it all," Wright complained.

"Let's light that candle."

Tom had sank into a chair and his cheek was on the table. Fargo touched him and Tom didn't move or respond.

It turned out Davenport had some lucifers in a belt pouch. He got the candle lit and Fargo had him hold it while he examined Tom's wound.

The slug had struck below the collarbone and exited near Tom's shoulder blade. The wound had bled a lot but now the blood had slowed to a trickle.

"I'm still waiting," Lieutenant Wright said, "and damned mad, I'll have you know."

Fargo handed the toothpick to Davenport. "Cut him down," he directed, and began to tug at Tom's buckskin shirt to get it off.

"I could use your help. I'm not as strong as you," Davenport said. "He might fall and hurt himself."

"Good," Fargo said. Between the blood and Tom's sweat, the shirt clung like a second skin. He had to wrestle it off. Tom didn't once move or open his eyes.

The thud of Wright striking the floor and the swearing that followed brought a fleeting grin.

"Sorry, sir," Private Davenport said. "I tried my best."

"I don't blame you," Lieutenant Wright said, stiffly rising and rubbing himself.

Just then Jacques Grevy let out with a shout.

"Americans! Do you think you are safe in there? If so, you are mistaken."

"That bastard," Lieutenant Wright said.

"The sun is coming up. It is the last sun you will ever see. Prepare yourselves, for soon all of you will die."

35

Mocking laughter told Fargo that Grevy was on the move. He'd like to slip out and deal with him but he had Tom to tend to first.

The chest of drawers wasn't locked. In it were a lot of female clothes, neatly folded: dresses, a chemise, skirts and shawls. There were also several work shirts and pants for a man. Underneath were towels and washcloths. He grabbed one of the towels.

Bear River Tom came around but he was too weak to even lift his head. When he saw what Fargo held, he said, "Pink?"

"It's the only color there was."

"Well, tits," Tom said. "I'm glad California Jim and Badger can't see me. They'd laugh me to death."

"Is there water in that?" Fargo asked Private Davenport, with a nod at a pitcher and basin.

"I'll check."

Lieutenant Wright had gone to the window and was peering out. "Where is he? I don't see that son of a bitch anywhere."

"I wouldn't do that," Fargo advised.

"I'm being careful," Wright said. He put his hand on the flap to his empty holster. "I wish the private and me had our guns. Grevy took them."

"You were lucky he left you alive."

"Maybe he figured if you didn't see us moving, you wouldn't come in the cabin."

Private Davenport returned with the pitcher. "There's about a cupful. That's all."

"It will have to do."

Fargo cleaned the wound, cut the towel into strips, and bandaged Tom's shoulder. The bleeding had about stopped by then. "It's the best I can do," he announced as he finished.

"Plumb decent of you," Tom said. "I'm afraid I won't be of much use, though."

"There's only one thing to do," Lieutenant Wright said. He was peering out the window again. "One of us has to ride to Fort Laramie and bring back reinforcements."

"I doubt that Grevy will let us leave, sir," Private Davenport said.

"We have to take care of him first, of course." Wright held out his hand toward Fargo. "Your revolver, if you please."

"No."

"I beg your pardon. I know Colonel Jennings said I was to pay heed to you but this is an emergency and I'm exercising my authority as an officer." Wright crooked his fingers. "I want your Colt."

"Not a chance in hell."

"Your rifle, then."

Fargo had leaned the Henry against the table before he cut Davenport down. Now he snatched it up and shook his head. "I'll need both. I'm going out there after him."

"I demand you obey me."

"Don't hold your breath," Fargo said, moving to the door.

"Arrogant, that's what you are," Wright said. "We should work together. I take your sidearm and you take your rifle and between the two of us, we put the quietus to Jacques Grevy. What could be simpler?"

"He won't die easy."

"Neither will we. Now hand that pistol over." In his agitation, Lieutenant Wright didn't realize he was holding a curtain partway open.

"Get away from there," Fargo cautioned. "You're a perfect target."

"Eh?" Wright faced the window and the back of his head exploded in a shower of hair, bone and blood. As if he were a puppet with its strings cut, he collapsed into a disjointed pile.

"Lieutenant!" Private Davenport cried, and started toward him.

With a quick bound Fargo grabbed his arm. "Stay away from that window."

Bear River Tom had turned his head and was sadly shaking it at the body. "That's the trouble with being so green."

"He was a good officer," Davenport said.

"No offense, boy," Tom replied, "but he was a jackass. Maybe with more experience he'd have amounted to something."

Off in the night, Jacques Grevy did more laughing. "Did I get him, *mon ami*? I very seldom miss."

Davenport opened his mouth to shout.

"Don't give him the satisfaction," Fargo said. He steered the young trooper over to the table. "I need you to keep an eye on Tom, here."

"What will you be doing?"

"What do you think?"

"Why not stay put? He can't shoot us if he can't see us."

"That's what the bastard wants," Fargo said. "To keep us pinned. Wait us out. Sooner or later hunger or thirst will drive us out and he'll pick us off. Or friends of his will show up and they'll set fire to the cabin and burn us out."

"What do I do while you're gone?"

"Protect Tom. If I don't come back, wait until nightfall and slip out and get to our horses. Tom knows where they are. It will be up to you to get him to the fort."

"I'm just a private."

"You're a soldier. You have your duty."

Fargo stared at Wright's body, then at the Henry, and thrust it at Davenport. "Here."

"What's going on. You wouldn't give it to the lieutenant. Why are you giving it to me?"

"He wanted to come out with me. You know enough to stay put." Drawing his Colt, Fargo moved to the door. He had a hunch Grevy was waiting for him to try something and was covering the front of the cabin.

"One last thing," Private Davenport said. "When he was hanging the lieutenant and me from the rafter, Grevy told us he was looking forward to pitting himself against you. He said you would be great sport."

Coiling, Fargo quietly worked the latch. "Let's find out."

36

Fargo pushed the door wide open. Almost instantly there was a shot, the bang of Grevy's rifle, but Fargo wasn't there. As he pushed he darted toward the window.

Lowering his head and shoulders, he dived at the lacy curtains. The window was wide enough that he hurtled clear through, tearing the curtains from their rod and taking them with him. He landed on his shoulder, rolled, and was up and around the corner of the cabin before Grevy's second shot boomed. It missed.

Squatting, Fargo cast a clinging curtain to the ground.

The golden curve of the sun was brightening the eastern sky. Soon it would be full light.

Fargo didn't dare stay in one place too long. Grevy would be stalking him. Whirling, he ran to the rear and on into the growth that bordered the stream. He worked his way along it, passing more tents, and came to another cabin.

Darting across a short open space, he glided to the right around the cabin to the front, and hunkered.

Golden hues painted the world's rim and the indigo of night was giving way to the azure of day. Here and there along the gulch birds were breaking into song and somewhere a jay squawked.

Fargo had second thoughts about leaving the Henry with Davenport. He should have left the Colt. At night a rifle wasn't much of an edge over a revolver but in the bright light of day it definitely was.

He scanned the rutted track that served as the settlement's street and the vegetation across the way but Grevy was too savvy to give himself away.

Turning, Fargo moved to a tent. He drew the Arkansas

toothpick and slashed, making an opening he could slip through. Once inside, he slid the toothpick back into its ankle sheath.

The flaps were tied back, and he peeked out.

Still no sign of Jacques Grevy.

In the tent were cots and two chests. There was also an iron stove with a pot belly, a heavy thing to lug halfway across the country in a wagon, but emigrants insisted on bringing the strangest things, from pianos to china cabinets.

The stove gave him an idea. Iron, after all, deflected lead.

Fargo darted over and crouched behind it. Taking off his hat, he watched the front.

Now all he could do was wait.

The light outside and inside brightened. A cat, of all things, wandered past, meowing.

Fargo didn't move. He was sure Grevy was hunting him. It was only a matter of time.

A half hour went by. More.

Fargo hoped Tom would be all right. He hoped young Davenport didn't show himself at the window or the door.

He hoped more of Laguerre's band didn't show up before he dealt with Grevy.

Fargo sensed movement before he saw it. Fingers appeared, but not at the front flap. They slid through the slit he'd cut in the side and the slit widened.

Fargo knew that Grevy was looking in. Grevy would see that the flaps were open and maybe figure he'd gone out the front.

He held his breath, waiting for Grevy to push through the opening. Instead, the fingers slid back and the slit closed.

Inwardly, Fargo swore. Did the one-eyed killer suspect he was in there? He trained the Colt on the front, his finger curled to the trigger.

Nothing happened. Grevy didn't appear.

Fargo wondered if Grevy had gone on and was searching farther up the gulch.

Without warning a flaming torch came sailing into the tent. It hit and skittered under a cot and almost went out but didn't. The flames grew, licking at the bottom. Smoke rose, and the cot caught fire.

Fargo jammed his hat on. So much for taking Grevy by surprise.

More smoke rose. It wouldn't be long before it filled the tent, making it impossible to breathe and forcing him out into the open. Exactly as Jacques Grevy wanted. Did Grevy know he was in there or was Grevy only guessing? It hardly mattered. He had to get out before the smoke became too thick.

Turning to the back, he pried at the bottom of the canvas, intending to raise it high enough to crawl out. Whoever had tied the tent down did a good job. He pulled with all his strength and raised it only an inch or so. He was about to holster the Colt and use both hands when a rifle spanged and lead ripped through the canvas a hand's width from his head.

Fargo moved toward the front.

The first cot crackled with flames that had spread to the second.

A log lay about twenty feet away outside the front flap. Fargo was girding himself to run to it when Grevy cut loose with shot after shot, raking the tent from end to end.

Fargo dropped flat. He waited for the shooting to stop, then was up and running. He bolted to the log and was prone behind it before Grevy could reload.

Had Grevy seen him? Fargo took off his hat again and inched his head up. A gun banged and slivers stung his cheek. Ducking, he jammed his hat on, twisted, and scrambled into the brush.

He rose to his hands and knees. He saw no sign of Grevy, and was about to head for the mouth of the gulch when he caught movement again.

Someone was stalking up the gulch from the other direction, moving smack down the middle of the track. It was Private Davenport, with the Henry. The youngster must think he was coming to help.

Fargo moved to intercept him. Grevy was bound to spot Davenport and drop him as easy as anything.

Davenport was glancing every which way but he couldn't look in every direction at once. He was almost to the tent Fargo had just escaped from when Jacques Grevy appeared from behind the one next to it with his rifle to his shoulder.

37

Fargo didn't have a clear shot at Grevy. Trees were in the way. He snapped a shot at him anyway and flew toward Davenport, yelling, "Take cover!"

The young private spun toward him and looked momentarily confused.

"Get down!" Fargo bawled just as Grevy's rifle belched smoke and sound.

Davenport stumbled and staggered and fell to his knees. Clutching his side, he tried to turn toward Grevy.

Fargo snapped off two more shots. He missed, but he came close enough that Grevy darted behind the tent. Bursting out of the undergrowth, he raced to Davenport, hooked an arm around him, and hoisted him to his feet.

"Hang on," he said, and retreated toward cover.

Grevy reappeared, taking aim, but Davenport fired and Grevy sprang back out of sight.

Davenport groaned.

Fargo got him behind a pine and eased him down. "How bad is it?"

"My side," Davenport said, gasping.

"Keep watch," Fargo directed, and knelt. A quick probe revealed that the slug had left a long and deep furrow along Davenport's ribs but hadn't penetrated his chest. "You were damned lucky."

"You call *this* luck?" Davenport doubled over.

"Why didn't you stay with Tom?"

Through clenched teeth, Davenport replied, "We were worried when we heard shots. Tom told me to come help you."

"By walking right out in the open?"

"I'm sorry. I wasn't thinking."

"You have grit, I'll say that," Fargo complimented him to lessen his embarrassment. "The general would be proud."

"My father might, at that."

Fargo took the Henry and made sure a round was in the chamber. He quickly reloaded the Colt and shoved it into Davenport's hand.

"What—?"

"To defend yourself," Fargo said. "We're swapping. Stay put. I'm going to draw him away."

"What if it doesn't work and he comes after me?"

"He can finish you off anytime," Fargo said. "I'm the one he really wants."

Davenport swallowed. "I won't go anywhere."

"You sure as hell better not." Fargo gave him a pat of encouragement and made for the tents, running all out. He knew Grevy was smart enough not to stay in the same spot for very long, and sure enough, as he burst into the clear, Grevy popped out from around a cabin farther down.

Grevy fired.

A hornet buzzed Fargo's ear. On the run he answered, jacked the lever, fired again. He reached the side of a tent. When he looked out, Grevy was gone.

The tent with the cots was burning. Flames leaped from the top, hissing and sizzling. Soon it would be engulfed. All it would take was a few gusts of wind to spread the fire to other tents and even the cabins, and the whole settlement would go up.

Fargo had a bigger concern: staying alive. Plowing through the greenery to the stream, he scrambled down the bank. He went about twenty yards, then climbed back up.

The tactic worked. Jacques Grevy was just coming around a cabin farther down.

Fargo jerked the Henry up but once again he didn't have a clear shot. The head or the heart, and he could finish this. Against strong temptation, he held his fire.

Grevy was a panther on the prowl. His head constantly swiveled, his one good eye raking everything. For most men having only one eye would be a handicap. Not for Grevy. He was as alert as an Apache.

Fargo fixed the Henry's sights on the killer's face just as a small spruce came between them. He expected Grevy to step past the tree. Then he would shoot.

Grevy didn't reappear.

Perplexed, Fargo crept closer. He figured his quarry had gone to ground but when he peered around the spruce, Grevy wasn't there.

Intuition caused Fargo to fling himself at the earth a heartbeat before Grevy's rifle blasted. Somehow Grevy had known right where he was.

Pushing up, Fargo darted toward a gap between two tents. He was almost to it when a rifle thundered and searing pain lanced his left arm. He ran to the front and bore to the right, racing thirty to forty feet before he sought cover again.

Grevy wasn't after him.

Hurriedly, Fargo examined his arm. The slug had clipped him, was all. He'd have a small scar to add to his collection, but he'd live.

Slowly rising onto his knees, he gazed up the gulch and then down it.

Not ten feet away Jacques Grevy was about to shoot.

Fargo fired his Henry from the hip. By a sheer fluke he struck Grevy's rifle, tearing it from the small man's grasp. He worked the lever but only had it halfway when Grevy was on him.

Grevy's knife flashed. Fargo blocked it with the Henry but the tip nicked his wrist. At close quarters the rifle was more a hindrance than a help, and he threw it at Grevy and leaped back.

Fargo whipped out the Arkansas toothpick. It was smaller and thinner than Grevy's knife but it wasn't the blade that counted as much as it was the skill of the blade's wielder. He parried a thrust and had the satisfaction of hearing Grevy swear.

Grevy didn't allow him a breather.

Fargo blocked, countered, was deflected. He feinted high and went low but Grevy wasn't fooled. Grevy feinted low and went high. Fargo barely smacked the steel away in time.

They crouched and circled, Grevy wagging his blade and grinning in smug confidence.

Fargo needed to goad him, to provoke him into being reckless. All he could think of, though, was something so childish, it was laughable. He sneered and said, "You fight like a girl."

And damned if it didn't work.

38

Jacques Grevy was a tornado before; now he was a hurricane. He rained blows. He stabbed and slashed and used every ploy in a knife fighter's bag of tricks.

Fargo was hard-pressed to stay alive. He was cut on the arm, on the shoulder. He lost skin on his neck. He tripped and would have died when Grevy thrust at his heart only his flailing arm struck Grevy's and knocked the knife aside.

Fargo had been in knife fights but never like this, never a fight so quick and so intense. Never, ever, had he gone up against someone as deadly as Jacques Grevy. He lost all sense of time, of self. There were the flashing blades and nothing else.

Then Grevy stabbed and kicked at the same time. Fargo dodged the knife but not the kick. His knee exploded in pain and his leg buckled. He braced his full weight on his other leg, and that was when Grevy pounced.

Fargo managed to grab Grevy's wrist. Grevy grabbed his. In their struggle they stumbled over the bank and suddenly empty space was below.

The shock of hitting the water, the splashing and the wet, disoriented Fargo, if only for a few seconds. He swiped at his eyes with his sleeve and as his vision cleared he saw Grevy lancing the knife at his throat. He parried with the toothpick.

The little man with the eye patch was tireless, a killer who didn't know the meaning of quit.

Grevy swung and Fargo countered but he was slowing. He could feel it and he knew that Grevy knew. Grevy was as confident as ever, his sneer never gone from his scarred face. And Grevy hadn't slowed a whit.

Pain seared Fargo's side, seared his thigh. He had been cut twice in the blink of an eye.

Fargo tried a last gambit. Blood oozing from his leg, he sagged and let his leg start to buckle.

Grevy took the bait. He sprang in, his knife poised, triumph lighting his dark eye.

With the speed of a striking rattler, Fargo drove the tip of the double-edged toothpick up and in, spearing it to the hilt under Grevy's jaw. Twisting, he wrenched, then sprang out of Grevy's reach.

It was well he did.

Grevy gurgled and growled, and with scarlet spewing from between his lips, he threw himself forward in a death stroke.

Fargo skipped back out of reach.

Grevy came down with a splash and didn't move. First one arm and then the other rose and then one leg and the other, and he floated facedown.

Backpedaling, Fargo gained the other bank. He fell onto his back and gasped. He was cut and nicked in a dozen places. Many were bleeding. Despite the cold, he was also covered with sweat. And his arms were leaden. He breathed in deep and willed the tension to drain from his body.

Jacques Grevy had been formidable. He'd come as close as anyone to sending Fargo into the hereafter.

Fargo lay and gazed at the sky and winced at the pain. When he heard splashing, he sat bolt upright, thinking that somehow Grevy was still alive and coming for him.

Private Davenport, holding the Colt, was wading across. He skirted Jacques Grevy's body, saying, "You did it, by God."

"Barely," Fargo said. "And you don't listen worth a damn."

"I had to come try and help," Davenport said. "I couldn't stay there and do nothing."

"The more I know you, the more you take after your old man," Fargo remarked. The general was well known for being a scrapper, and for always putting the welfare of his men before all else.

"I suppose I do, at that," Davenport said thoughtfully. "More than I imagined." He sat and touched his side, and grimaced. "It hurts like hell."

"You'll live."

"And so will your friend Tom," Davenport said. "But now there's just you and him and me, and all three of us are hurt."

"I'm hurt the least," Fargo said, "which is why the two of you are heading for Fort Laramie before the day is out."

"What will you do?"

"Do you even have to ask?"

Davenport shook his head. "You can't take them all on alone. There are too many."

"It's not as bad as you think. Some of his own people are against him."

"Even so. Consider the odds."

"If I did that all the time," Fargo said, "I'd have given up scouting and become a store clerk years ago."

"I should go with you."

"No."

"I can help."

"No, damn it." Fargo looked at him. "Listen to me. That tit-crazed lunkhead in the cabin is a friend. I don't have any I can spare, so I want you to look after him and see that he makes it to the fort and get him to the doc."

"I don't like leaving you to tangle with them by your lonesome."

"You want some of the glory, is that it?" Fargo asked sarcastically.

"Hell, no," young Davenport said. He gestured at Grevy. "There's no glory in that. No glory in violence at all. It's ugly. It's brutal."

"You're learning," Fargo said.

Davenport looked at his side. "The hard way. It's made me think. I see my father in a whole new light." He paused. "He was right and I was wrong. He doesn't lord it over his men just because he's an officer."

"I could have told you that."

"I always saw him barking commands. Having his men do this and do that. All that training he made them go through. He did it to keep them alive when they run up against something like this."

"Good officers do what they can."

"He didn't go to West Point just to bark orders. He went

to become the best officer he could be and keep those under him alive."

Fargo was thinking of all the stitching his buckskins would need. He hated spending hours with a needle and sinew.

"Why didn't I see that before?" Private Davenport asked.

"Sometimes life has to kick us in the head to get our attention."

Davenport grimaced. "The lieutenant, dead. All the other troopers, dead. Your friend, badly wounded. Me hurt and you cut up. This was some kick."

"It sure was," Fargo agreed.

39

Fargo had a feeling. A bad feeling. Call it gut instinct or call it intuition. He about rode the Ovaro into the ground.

Buzzards were the first sign his gut was right.

Over a score of the big, black, ugly scavengers were pinwheeling in the sky.

The Metis had broken camp. The fires had been put out, the tents taken down, the wagons and the carts were gone.

All that was left were the bodies. The settlers lay sprawled in the throes of their violent ends. Every last man, woman and child had been massacred and left to rot.

Fargo sat his saddle and watched the vultures peck and pick and a great fury seized him. A wrath so great, he shook from head to toe.

There were too many for him to bury. Nature would have to take its grisly course. The buzzards would feast, and the coyotes and others would come out at night to feed, and inside of a week there would be little but torn clothes and picked-clean bones.

Laguerre's band had headed north toward far-distant Canada and home.

"You'll get there over my dead body," Fargo vowed.

Intent on following the trail and still boiling mad over the slaughter, he didn't pay as much attention as he should to the surrounding slopes. Not until the Ovaro raised its head and whinnied.

He wasn't the only one to see the vultures. So had a Sioux war party. Seven warriors swept out of the far timber and raced toward him with whoops and yells.

"Damn." Fargo hauled on the reins. This was the last thing he needed. He had no wish to tangle with the Lakotas.

They were only defending their territory. But he doubted they'd listen to reason. He was white. That was enough for them to count coup on him.

Using his spurs, he reached the forest before the warriors were in bow range. He had to lose them but once the Sioux were on a scent they were like bloodhounds. They might chase him for days. He couldn't afford that. Nothing must keep him from catching up to the Laguerres.

Fargo climbed, the steep slopes slowing the stallion.

But the slopes would also slow the Sioux.

He considered an easy way to stop them. Stop and dismount and as soon as they were close enough, open up with the Henry. He didn't need to shoot the warriors. All he had to do was bring down their mounts.

The thing was, he had an aversion to killing horses. He only ever did it as a last resort.

So he climbed and sought a way to stop them without killing them or their animals, and had about resigned himself to doing what he didn't want to when, lo and behold, a deadfall appeared.

As deadfalls went, it was small. Heavy rain or strong winds or both had uprooted twenty or thirty middling-sized trees and now they were in a jumble, many of their limbs broken and missing.

Quickly, he reined around and up until he was above the fall. Vaulting from the saddle, he did what no one with any common sense would do. He clambered out onto the trees.

He came to a fir perched precariously on top of the others. Putting his back to it, he pushed. It moved. Not much, but it moved.

The Sioux were howling like wolves. And like wolves, they were hard after him, making for the deadfall. As yet, none of them had spotted him on top of it.

Fargo gauged the distance and how fast they were climbing, and when the moment was right, he pushed again, his body as taut as a wire. The fir slid a little ways and stopped. He strained until he was fit to bust a gut but it wouldn't move any farther. Then he saw why. A stub of a branch was caught. To climb over and try to break it or chop it with the toothpick would take too long. The war party would reach him before he could dislodge it.

So Fargo pushed harder. He grit his teeth and thrust with his legs and after a few seconds the tree slid but nowhere near enough.

Fargo had time for one more try. He hooked his hands underneath the tree, bent, and heaved.

Below the deadfall, the bloodthirsty banshees rapidly closed.

The tree canted. The stub cracked and shattered and the tree was loose.

Fargo went on pushing. The fir lifted and tumbled over those under it, gaining momentum as it went. Like a rolling snowball that became an avalanche or a dislodged rock that created a talus slide, the fir dislodged others.

The lead warrior drew rein, startled. He looked back at the others and pointed and shouted. To a man, they came to a stop. And then, with trees crashing and clattering toward them, they wheeled their horses and fled.

Fargo did some fleeing of his own. He was well up on the mountain before the din from below faded. On reaching a ridge he checked his back trail.

The Sioux were a quarter of a mile or more lower down and not climbing nearly as swiftly as before. They recognized a lost cause.

Fargo rode on. He was over the crest before nightfall and made cold camp midway down. From his vantage he could see for miles across the prairie and nowhere was there so much as a point of light.

That was all right. Wagons and carts could go only so fast. Especially laden with gold and spoils.

Fargo sharpened the toothpick and thought of what he would do when he overtook them.

One way or the other, Anton and Marie would pay. One way or the other, there would be a reckoning.

And by God—and his Colt and his Henry—it would be written in their blood.

40

From far off the campfires gave the illusion of being so many fireflies.

Fargo slowed the Ovaro to a walk. He had ridden since dawn, stopping only twice to rest the stallion.

Caution was called for. Their dogs or their horses might catch his scent. He made sure that he was downwind as he drew closer.

Their wagons and carts were in a circle. Women hovered over supper pots. Children helped or played. The men were huddled around the fires or in small groups, talking.

Fargo came to a stop. Something wasn't right. He studied the camp and finally it came to him.

"What the hell?" he said out loud.

Puzzled, he circled the circle. He counted the wagons and carts to be sure and counted the Metis to be doubly sure.

For half an hour he sat and watched. Finally he raised his reins and clucked to the Ovaro and boldly made for the wagons. It wasn't until the flickering firelight played over his hat that a boy spotted him and shouted an alarm. Drawing rein, he leaned on his saddle horn.

Men were grabbing rifles and rushing to the barrier while the women gathered their children and moved toward the middle.

Muzzles were trained on him but lowered at a command from a figure who shouldered through to the tongue of a wagon and placed his foot on it. "You," he said simply.

"Claude," Fargo replied.

"We were expecting soldiers," Claude said.

"I saw the bodies."

"Things are not as they were," Claude informed him.

"I can see that."

"Would you care for some coffee? Or something to eat? I assure you that you are in no danger. Not from us, anyway."

"I should be pushing on," Fargo said.

"We have a few questions we would ask," Claude said. "You need not worry you will lose them. They are not that far ahead."

Anxiety was stamped on every face, men and women and even the children.

"I reckon some coffee would do me right fine," Fargo allowed.

Claude had several men lift the tongue so the Ovaro could ride through. He led Fargo to a fire and Fargo climbed down and put a hand to the small of his back.

"You have spent many hours in the saddle, *oui*?"

"Been riding like hell," Fargo said.

Claude motioned at a woman and spoke in French and she came over and filled a tin cup with steaming coffee and timidly passed it to Fargo. "We do not have cream but we do have sugar."

"Black is fine." Fargo was aware that the others had surrounded him and were anxiously observing his every movement. "Your friends seem a mite nervous."

"They are worried for themselves and their families," Claude said, and gestured. "Please, make yourself comfortable." He sat cross-legged with his elbows on his knees.

Fargo hunkered. He made it a point to hold the tin cup in his left hand and keep his right near his holster.

"I spoke the truth when I said things are different," Claude said.

"I'm listening," Fargo said.

Those Metis who could speak English were translating for those who couldn't.

"It was, as you Americans would say, the last straw," Claude said, and a haunted look came over him.

Fargo sipped and waited.

"It started when you escaped. Marie was furious. You had humiliated her, and she was out for your blood."

"Anton?"

"He was worried. He said that Jacques Grevy should have

been back, that something must have happened to him. That it could well be that the soldiers had sent for reinforcements."

"What did Marie say to that?"

"She became worried. Over her gold, not anything else. She wouldn't risk losing it. So she gave the order to pack up and prepare to depart."

"And the settlers?"

Claude's face clouded with misery. "She said that they would speak against us in your courts. That we could not take them with us because they would slow us down. That only left one thing."

"Killing them."

Claude swallowed and nodded. "Some of us spoke against it. We said there were women and children, and no Metis would do such a thing."

"She had them killed anyway."

"Not right away. She was clever about it. She told us that she would think it over and make up her mind in the morning. So most of us went to sleep." Claude raised a hand to his eyes as if to hide the sight he'd beheld. "It was about midnight when the first shots woke us. The shots and the screams. We scrambled from our blankets and ran to where the settlers were tied but it was too late."

"Marie had them gunned down."

"*Oui.* Those who blindly follow Marie and Anton, what is asked of them, they do. Some of us were outraged and told her what she had done was terrible beyond belief. Can you guess what she did? She laughed in our faces. When some of our women broke into tears, she laughed at them, as well."

"And Anton?"

"He was eager to leave. To be honest, with all those bodies, so were we. But we were mad, many of us. Madder than we had ever been. And this afternoon, when we reached this very spot, we marched up to them and told them enough was enough."

"About damn time."

Claude nodded. "The shame, it is almost more than we can bear."

Fargo saw it on every face, in every eye.

"We told Marie and Anton that we wanted nothing more to do with them. Anton drew his pistol and threatened to kill anyone who defied them. To our surprise, Marie told him to leave us alone, that if we thought it best to go our separate ways, she would go along with our wishes."

Fargo could guess her real reason. The gold. Most likely she'd return to Canada and disappear. Maybe assume a new name. If they were careful and smart, no one would ever connect them with the massacre.

"So we split up," Claude was saying. "Only seven men went with Marie and Anton, the same seven who helped them slaughter the captives. Three are married with families."

Fargo frowned. "Women and sprouts." That complicated things.

"Three wives, eight children. I know for a fact that two of the wives do not agree with what their husbands are doing."

"I'm obliged for the information."

"I am happy to help." Claude looked earnestly at him. "Now we need information from you. Will your army come after us? Will they punish us for what the others have done?"

"No."

"You are sure?"

"When I get back to Fort Laramie, I'll tell Colonel Jennings how things were."

"Begging your pardon, what if you don't make it back? Marie and Anton are accomplished killers, the pair of them."

"The soldiers fight shy of the Black Hills. Even if they find the bodies, they won't come this far after you. The rest of you should have nothing to fear."

Translations brought more than a few smiles of relief.

"We are most happy to hear this," Claude said. "I am just sorry we didn't stand up to Marie and Anton sooner."

"I bet those settlers were sorry, too."

Claude winced as if he had been struck. "We will have nightmares about them for the rest of our lives."

"Good," Fargo said.

"You are a hard man, *monsieur.*"

"Not hard enough." Fargo regretted not killing Marie when he had the chance. If he had, the settlers might be alive. Draining the last of his coffee, he stood. "I have riding to do."

"One last thing, if you please."

Fargo had turned but stopped.

"Marie expects you to come after them. I heard her say they must be ready."

"Us Americans have another saying," Fargo said. "Ready or not, here I come."

41

It was so obvious, it was almost laughable.

As another dawn broke over the vastness of the prairie, Fargo lay on his belly on a grassy rise overlooking a broad bend in a stream. Cottonwoods and plant life grew heavy along its banks, affording plenty of cover.

The Laguerres and their followers had made camp in the bend. On three sides they were hemmed by water. On the fourth, facing the prairie, they had parked their wagons and carts.

For him to get at them, he either had to cross open grassland or else cross the ten-to-twelve-foot-wide stream.

Either way, he'd be a sitting—or moving—duck.

Fargo debated. They were bound to have men posted at the wagons and in the trees. He couldn't just go charging in.

A single fire sent wisps of smoke skyward. Around it sat the three women and eight children Claude had mentioned. There wasn't a man to be seen. Nor any sign of Marie and Anton.

"They must reckon I'm dumb as hell," Fargo said out loud. Below him, the weary Ovaro stood half dozing.

The way Fargo saw it, he had three choices. The first was to wait them out. In four or five days they might figure he wasn't coming and move on, and he could hit them when they were strung out and vulnerable.

Or he could go down there and give that bitch and her pussy-whipped husband what they deserved.

Or he could do what he now did. Sliding down the rise, he climbed on the Ovaro. "Sorry, big fella," he said. He rode west until he was out of sight of the camp. Then he rode to the stream.

He let the stallion drink but stayed on. When he judged it had enough, he made his way to the east until he was about two hundred yards from the bend. Dismounting, he tied the reins, yanked the Henry from the scabbard, and crept forward.

Living with the Sioux and tangling with the Apaches and others had taught him a few things. How to move slow and silent and blend in. How to use an enemy's habits against them.

Take whites, for instance. Few white men could sit or lie still for any length of time. They fidgeted. They scratched. They coughed.

So when Fargo reached a log on the west bank of the stream, he removed his hat, rested his chin on the ground, and didn't move a muscle for half an hour.

In that time he spotted two of them.

One was in a thicket. If he hadn't raised a hand to his face to brush away a bug, Fargo wouldn't have known he was there.

The other was in the fork of a tree. Thankfully, he was looking the other way when Fargo snaked to the log. He gave himself away when he coughed.

That accounted for two of the seven men Claude said were with the Laguerres.

Fargo discovered two more, thanks to a thoughtful woman. He'd glance at the camp every now and then, and along about noon he saw a woman rise from the fire and carry food on a plate to the rear of a parked wagon. She said something and a man's hand reached down and took the plate. She returned to the fire for a second plate, which she took to a different wagon.

That made four of the seven.

Fargo figured at least two more were somewhere along the far bend of the stream. So only one was unaccounted for.

He didn't see Marie or Anton anywhere.

Moving slowly so as not to draw the attention of the man in the tree, Fargo brought the Henry to bear. He reminded himself that these were the bastards who had taken part in the slaughter, fixed a bead on the man's ear and fired.

Working the lever, Fargo sat up.

The man in the thicket had done the same and was looking all around, trying to pinpoint where the shot came from.

Fargo shot him in the head.

At the fire a woman hollered and a young girl screamed.

The two men in the wagons barreled out. One spotted the broken body of the man who had fallen from the tree. He pointed and the pair started toward him.

Firing smoothly, methodically, Fargo put a slug into each of their brainpans.

Somewhere a man shouted, and the undergrowth crackled. Two more burst from a cluster of saplings. They stood back-to-back, their rifles raised.

They might as well have painted bull's-eyes on their temples.

Fargo expected the last man and the Laguerres would be smart and stay hidden. He was considerably surprised when, after about fifteen minutes, an older man appeared holding a long stick with a dirty white handkerchief tied to the end of it.

The man waved the stick with one hand and held the other open shoulder-high to show he was unarmed.

Suspecting a trick, Fargo stayed where he was.

The old man went to the north side of the bend and stood waving his stick a while. He called out, *"Monsieur Éclaireur!"* a few times. Then he turned and came to the near side and did the same.

Fargo took a risk. He raised his head and shoulders over the log and aimed at the man's face. "Looking for me?"

The old man gave a start. He was pasty with sweat and near white with fear. *"Oui,"* he stammered.

Fargo held the Henry rock steady while scouring the growth for Marie and Anton. "Where are they?" he snapped.

The old man didn't ask who he meant. He replied, "Gone, *monsieur.*"

"Like hell," Fargo growled.

"My English," the old man said, "it is not so good. They went with the gold." He pointed his stick to the north. "They leave us to slow you."

Damned if Fargo didn't think he was telling the truth. It sounded like something the Laguerres would do.

"S'il vous plaît," the old man said. "You go after them, yes?"

"What about you?" Fargo said.

"Me, *monsieur*?"

"Did you have a hand in the killing?"

"Killing, *monsieur*?"

"Don't play dumb."

The old man's throat bobbed. "You mean the settlers, yes?"

"You helped massacre them."

"No, *monsieur*. It was the others. Not me."

"You're a lying son of a bitch."

The old man trembled and became even whiter. "Where is your proof?"

"Your face," Fargo said.

The old man touched his cheek and said, *"Mon Dieu."*

Fargo stroked the trigger.

Rising, he jammed his hat on and glanced at the huddled women and children. Some were crying.

"Hell," he said.

42

The tracks of one wagon and a single cart, with a horse tied to the side of the wagon, pointed due north. The wagon was three times the size of the cart yet the cart's wheels sank deeper.

"I wonder why," Fargo said. He had been following them for hours now.

The Laguerres were pushing their teams almost cruelly. Greed did that. They pushed so hard that when Fargo came to the top of a knoll and saw the cart on its side and furniture and other effects scattered around it, he wasn't surprised.

A wheel had given out. It couldn't take all that weight, and several spokes had broken.

Apparently Anton and Marie didn't have spares because they'd transferred the gold from the cart to the wagon. To make room, they'd thrown out some of her furniture and the bearskin rug.

They'd continued north.

Sunset was gorgeous. Other times, other places, Fargo would have admired it. Now he had eyes only for the tracks. He was worried darkness would descend before he caught up.

The encroaching twilight brought the coyotes out.

Once, the Ovaro suddenly raised its head and stared to the east with its ear pricked. Fargo looked and listened but didn't see or hear anything.

Just when it became too dark to see and he thought he'd have to stop, a finger of orange and red broke the blackness.

They'd made no effort to hide their fire. That told him something right there.

The wagon sat with the tongue up. Horses were tied to its wheels and tailgate.

A teapot had been heated and a cup was in Marie's lap. She wore an ankle-length dress and had fluffed her hair and acted for all the world as if she were at a lady's social and not in the middle of nowhere.

Fargo drew rein. It would be foolish to ride on in. It would be beyond foolish. Yet after studying the wagon, that was what he did.

Marie didn't cry out or jump up in alarm. As calmly as you please, she took a sip of tea. Then, as he came to a stop, she smiled pleasantly and said, "I knew you would come. I knew it as surely as I have ever known anything."

"Where is he?" Fargo asked.

"Perhaps he is in the wagon," she said, grinning.

"There were two horses pulling the wagon and one pulling the cart and one tied to the side of the wagon, besides." Fargo tallied their animals up. "That makes four."

"And now there are only three," Marie said. "How clever of you."

"Where is he?" Fargo asked again.

"Would you believe me if I said he took most of the gold and deserted me?"

Fargo shook his head.

"*Non*, eh?"

"I'm not as stupid as you'd like me to be, bitch."

"Here now," Marie said. "The least you can do is be civil."

"Lady," Fargo said, "the least I can do is not gun you where you sit."

"Why haven't you?"

"Where is he?"

Marie let out an exaggerated sigh. "You sink your teeth into something and you don't let go."

"All those men, women and children," Fargo said.

"What else was I to do? Their testimony could have me hung."

"Instead it will be a bullet to the brain."

"You can do that? If I sit here and don't lift a finger against you?" Marie shook her head. "I think not. I am a shrewd judge of men and I think you have too much character to kill like that."

"Now we know who's the stupid one," Fargo said.

"I am trying to be nice."

"I'm not."

Her brow puckered and she said, "There is one thing I do not understand."

"Just one?"

"You knew he was not here yet you rode in anyway. What if he was lying off in the dark with a rifle?"

"He's not."

"How can you be so certain?"

"The missing horse," Fargo said. As well as earlier when the Ovaro had heard something to the east.

"Ah." Marie sipped and held the china cup in both hands. "I told him not to go but he wouldn't listen. He's done it four times now."

"He circles back to see if there's any sign of me and maybe catch me by surprise."

"Oui."

"It might have worked if he'd timed it right," Fargo said. "He circled past me and didn't know it."

"Men," Marie said bitterly. "They are next to worthless."

"You found a use for him."

"I did, didn't I?" Marie said, and laughed. "He thinks he is so clever. I have him wrapped around my finger. I have only to say do this or do that and he does it."

"Brag, why don't you?"

"He loves me, you know. The poor, simple fool truly loves me."

"Some gents can't tell shit from a rose," Fargo said.

Marie colored, and her right hand dipped to her side. "Now you go too far."

"We're taking this all the way," Fargo said. "And you damn well know it."

"You don't intend to hold me here until he returns?"

"You'll be here," Fargo said. "You just won't be breathing."

"How sure of yourself you are."

Fargo didn't reply.

"I am curious," Marie said. "If it is you, what will you do with the gold?"

Until that moment Fargo hadn't given it any thought. "I reckon I'll turn it over to the army." Most of it, anyway. He might keep a saddlebag full. There was a high-stakes poker game down to Saint Louis he'd like to take part in.

"Then you are the stupid one, after all." Marie thought about it and added, "Or a paragon of virtue."

"Any virtues I have," Fargo said, "I try to ignore them. All I am is a man you pissed off, and you shouldn't have."

"You make it sound personal," Marie said. "What were they to you? Did you know some of them?"

Fargo shook his head.

"You go to all this trouble for strangers? You are ready to kill for strangers?"

"Already have," Fargo said.

She arched an eyebrow.

"The rest of your men."

"All of them?"

"*Oui*, as you'd say."

"I thought perhaps you had gone around them. You got here so quickly." Marie casually moved her right hand into the folds of her dress.

"Times like these," Fargo said, "I half wish I was an Apache."

"Why?"

"So I could carve on you before you died. Cut off your nose. Dig out your eyeballs. Stick a knife between your legs."

"Goodness, you are vicious."

"You slaughtered little kids, you goddamn bitch."

"Ah. So that is the gist of this. You resent the innocents."

"I resent you," Fargo said, and put his hand on his Colt. "If you're going to do it, do it. Quit talking me to death in the hope I'll make it easy for you."

"So," she said grimly. "It is the moment of truth, as they say."

Fargo watched her right hand and only her right hand.

Marie looked at the wagon. "All that gold. All that lovely, wonderful gold." And her hand swept out with a derringer already cocked.

Fargo drew and shot her between her breasts. The impact smashed her back and the china cup fell. She gamely tried to straighten and raise the derringer, and he shot her between the eyes.

In the silence that followed, the crackling of the fire was like thunder.

Fargo reloaded. Dismounting, he tied the Ovaro to the wagon. He slid the Henry from the scabbard and used it to prop Marie's body so that it appeared she was sitting at the fire as he had first seen her, her chin to her chest. Then he went to the wagon and lay under it to wait.

Anton must have gone a considerable distance. It was a while before hooves pounded and he came racing out of the night, caution thrown to the wind in his concern for the woman who had led him around like a bull with a ring in its nose. He slowed when he saw her and then came on fast again, not realizing the trick that was being played on him.

"Big and dumb," Fargo said to himself.

In a swirl of dust Anton reined to a stop and was out of the saddle before his horse stopped moving. "Marie!" he cried. "I heard shots." He looked all around and finally looked at her and saw the Henry and took a step back. *"Non!"*

By then Fargo had eased unnoticed out from under the wagon and took a step to the right to be clear of it. "Yes," he said.

Anton spun, his huge hand splayed over his revolver. "You!"

"Who the hell else would it be?"

"You killed her."

"With great pleasure," Fargo said.

"Bastard," Anton hissed.

"More than I felt when she made love to me."

"Pig of a pig." Anton glowered and bunched his fists. "I tell you what, American. Let's settle this man to man. Just you and me. No guns. No knives. We throw them away and we fight until one of us is dead."

"Sure," Fargo said. "And while I'm at it, why don't I get down on my knees and put my hands in my pockets?"

"You have no honor."

"Coming from you," Fargo said, "that's a laugh."

Anton glanced at Marie, and drew. His hand was rising when a slug from Fargo's Colt smashed his knuckles. Blood spurted, and his revolver clattered at his feet. Clutching himself, he spat, "No one is that fast."

Fargo shot him in the left knee.

Crying out, Anton staggered. "Get it over with, damn you."

Fargo shot him in the right knee.

Another cry, and Anton was down, his good hand under him, hissing and glaring and quaking with raw hate. "Why do you do this?"

Fargo pointed the Colt.

"I die willingly, American. I go to join the woman I love."

"You two are enough to make me hope there's really a hell."

"So we will suffer forever?" Anton laughed.

"See if you think this is funny," Fargo said, and shot him in the face.

After the bulk stopped convulsing, Fargo reclaimed his Henry, dragged Marie over to Anton, and dumped her on top of him.

Hitching the team took a while. He got under way and looked back at the lumps of nothing.

"The buzzards should thank me," Fargo said, and flicked the reins.

It was a long way to Fort Laramie.

LOOKING FORWARD!
The following is the opening section of the next novel in the exciting *Trailsman* series from Signet:

TRAILSMAN #384
DIABLO DEATH CRY

The Southwest Trail (Texas and New Mexico), 1861—where Skye Fargo sets out to make a few easy dollars and gets caught in a deadly web of conspiracy and treason.

The words had plagued Skye Fargo's mind since he had headed south from Red River to start this new job: *Wait for what will come.*

That was how Hernando Quintana had ended his first dispatch to Fargo. And what eventually came was a new chamois pouch filled with five hundred dollars in gold double eagles—and a promissory note for five hundred more at the completion of the job.

That was way too much money. And Fargo had learned long ago that when men overpaid him, it generally meant he was going to be the meat that feeds the tiger.

Wait for what will come.

"The story of my life," Fargo muttered.

"The hell are you mumbling, catfish?" demanded the man mountain blocking out the sun on Fargo's left. "Speak up like you own a pair!"

Excerpt from DIABLO DEATH CRY

Fargo and his recently hired companion, Bill "Booger" McTeague, were riding through the flat saw-grass country of the Gulf Coast in east Texas. On their left, the metallic blue water of the Gulf of Mexico stretched out to infinity, furling waves beating themselves into cotton foam as they crashed onto the white sand beach.

Fargo reined in his black-and-white stallion and shaded his lake-blue eyes with one hand, taking a careful squint ahead and behind. He sat tall in the saddle, a broad-shouldered, narrow-hipped, crop-bearded man dressed in fringed buckskins. A dust-darkened white hat left most of his weather-bronzed face in shadow.

"What I said," Fargo finally replied, "is that the two of us will soon be up against it. The back of my neck has been tingling for the past hour."

"Pah!" Booger loosed a brown streamer into the knee-high grass. "Pull up your skirts, Nancy! All you jaspers with pretty teeth are squeamish. Why, this job is money for old rope. We may have to kill a Comanch or two, and p'r'aps a few Apaches will try to blow out our wicks, is all."

Fargo gigged the Ovaro forward again after loosening his Henry repeater in its saddle boot.

"We'll be hugging with red aborigines, all right," he said. "You can't avoid them on the southern route into California. And these Southwest tribes can't be bought off with tribute like the ones up north. Matter of fact, we're being watched right now—and there's a tribe in this area, the Karankawas, known to be cannibals."

At this startling intelligence, Booger's head snapped toward Fargo. "No Choctaw here, catfish. Is that the straight word?"

Fargo's lips twitched into a grin. Booger's moon face looked more curious than frightened. The shaggy giant was six foot five inches tall and weighed two hundred and eighty-five pounds. His prodigious bulk forced him to ride a saddle-ox on long rides like this one. He was thick in the chest and waist, his arms bigger around the wrists than most brawny men were in the forearms. He wore a floppy hat and butternut-

dyed shirt and trousers with knee-length elk-skin moccasins.

"It is," Fargo replied. "But it's not cannibals watching us,
old son."

"Fargo, you double-poxed hound, I am not the lad for rid-
dles. Who is it?"

Again the ominous words snapped in Fargo's mind like
burning twigs: *Wait for what will come.*

"I don't have the foggiest notion in hell," he admitted.
"But I suspect it's somebody who's been expecting us, and I
doubt if they mean to invite us to a cider party."

Booger threw back his head and howled like a wolf.
"Faugh! A good set-to makes my pecker hard. Put a name to
it and I will kill it. Nerve up, you little pipsqueak. Say! Old
Booger used to whip an Overland swift wagon on the San
Antonio Road. There is a fine whorehouse at Powder Horn.
We can get liquored up and plant our carrots before we even
report to these Dagos."

"Clean your ears or cut your hair. I think somebody's lay-
ing for us. No frippet and no carouse until we puzzle this
deal out."

Booger looked mortally offended.

"Fargo, when did you become so old maidish? I do not
require your permission to top a hot little senyoreeter."

"You do as long as you're working for me, you mammoth
ape. I put you on the payroll because Quintana demanded
the best driver I could find. But I *won't* take your damn
guff."

"No need to get your bowels in an uproar. Gerlong there,
Ambrose!" Booger called to his saddle-ox. "G'long there,
whoop!"

At first Fargo had been skeptical of Ambrose. But
although the huge, placid beast could not move at a fast clip,
he could cover twenty-four miles in four hours even in heavy
sand. The Ovaro had quickly accepted the good-natured
animal, and in any event the only alternative for a man of
Booger's size was a conveyance and team.

Fargo's startling blue eyes stayed in constant scanning

motion despite the flat, open terrain. He especially paid attention to the Ovaro's delicately veined ears. They were often the first indication of potential trouble.

Ten minutes passed in silence, each man alone with his thoughts. Then:

"This Espanish hombre," Booger said. "The hell's his name again?"

"Hernando Quintana."

"Is he one a them whatchacallits—grandees?"

"Nah. He was a viceroy until the Mexican revolution."

"The hell's a viceroy?"

The Ovaro's ears twitched. Eyes slitted against the bright sunlight, Fargo took another good squint around them.

"It's a fellow who governs a province for the Spanish king," he finally replied. "This one was in charge of Monterrey, Mexico. A lot of 'em were killed when the revolution broke out, but this Quintana escaped to New Orleans."

Booger grunted. He hawked up phlegm, spat, then said sarcastically, "Bully for him. Them garlics gripe my nuts. It's them bastards that taught the featherheads to scalp and torture."

"Never mind the soapbox," Fargo said, watching the brisk Gulf breeze ripple through the tall saw grass in waves. "Just keep a weather eye out for trouble. We're both hanging out here exposed like a set of dog balls."

"Teach your grandmother to suck eggs, nervous Nellie! Why, a titmouse couldn't sneak up on us in country this open and flat."

Fargo couldn't gainsay that. But years of frontier survival had taught him how danger sometimes gave the air a certain texture. And he felt that texture now—a galvanic charge like the one he sometimes felt just before a massive crack of thunder and lightning.

Booger gnawed off a corner of plug. When he had it juicing good he parked it in his cheek and said, "Say, catfish . . . will there be any women in this Dago's party?"

"He mentioned his daughter."

"Ha-ho, ha-ho! A daughter, and he hires on the Trailsman?

Oh, Lulu girl! You'll have her ankles behind her ears before next breakfast."

Fargo let out a long, fluming sigh. "Booger, you ain't got enough brains to have a headache. Now you lissenup: Spaniards are known for taking quick offense. I want you to mind your manners around them, hear? You keep a civil tongue in your head. And Christsakes, *don't* be spying on the women when they bathe. That's a dangerous habit and will get you shot someday."

"Pipe down, you jay. Easy for you to say—you've seen more quiff than a midwife. Old Booger ain't had a woman in so long he's forgot what the gash that never heals looks like."

Fargo snorted. "Somebody get me a violin."

Within the next hour the two riders reached the northeast shore of Matagorda Bay. Powder Horn, a jumping-off settlement a few miles inland, marked the beginning of a good wagon road that had been well traveled since the army built it in 1849. Fargo was to join the Quintana party there.

They turned west onto a narrow trace that led past windswooped palm trees and gigantic live oaks draped in graygreen curtains of Spanish moss. Fargo considered this part of Texas an extension of the Deep South but far more dangerous: Law was scarce and gangs of ruthless *contrabandistas* controlled the region, part of the smuggling operations that flourished all along the western Gulf of Mexico.

The giant, spreading limbs overhead blocked much of the sunlight, and the wide-boled trees themselves made for an ambusher's paradise. The Ovaro, used to wide open country and good visibility, stutter-stepped nervously now and then—like Fargo he didn't take to being hemmed in.

Fargo had jerked his brass-framed Henry from its saddle scabbard and now rode with it balanced across his left arm. Booger, rocking sideways on his loose-skinned saddle-ox, kept his cap-and-ball Colt's Dragoon to hand.

"This place is heap bad medicine," he remarked. "Too damn quiet, hey? No bird noises, no insect hum. Quiet as the grave. Gives old Booger the fantods."

Fargo had noticed the same thing. The stillness was so complete it seemed to scream.

Again, the unwelcome words nagged his memory like the tag end of a song he hated but could not shake: *Wait for what will come. . . . Wait. . . .*

The trace narrowed even more and Fargo gigged the Ovaro ahead so the men could ride single file. A carpet of leathery oak leaves covered the trace.

"Two more miles and we'll break into open tableland," Fargo said. "If we—"

The Trailsman never finished his sentence. The Ovaro, moving forward at a slow, steady trot, planted his left forefoot, then suddenly plummeted toward the ground.

Fargo, caught completely by surprise, jerked his feet from the stirrups. His first thought was that his stallion had stepped into a gopher hole, and Fargo didn't want his legs trapped when the Ovaro fell.

But this "hole," Fargo quickly realized when both of the Ovaro's forelegs were swallowed up, was a man-made pitfall trap. The leaf-covered framework of boughs collapsed, and Fargo pitched forward hard over his pommel—straight toward three pointed stakes smeared black with deadly poison!

THE LAST OUTLAWS
The Lives and Legends of Butch Cassidy and the Sundance Kid

by Thom Hatch

Butch Cassidy and the Sundance Kid are two of the most celebrated figures of American lore. As leaders of the Wild Bunch, also known as the Hole-in-the-Wall Gang, they planned and executed the most daring bank and train robberies of the day, with an uprecedented professionalism.

The Last Outlaws brilliantly brings to life these thrilling, larger-than-life personalities like never before, placing the legend of Butch and Sundance in the context of a changing—and shrinking—American West, as the rise of 20th century technology brought an end to a remarkable era. Drawing on a wealth of fresh research, Thom Hatch pushes aside the myth and offers up a compelling, fresh look at these icons of the Wild West.

**Available wherever books are sold or at
penguin.com**

No other series packs this much heat!

THE TRAILSMAN

Follow the trail of Penguin's Action Westerns at
penguin.com/actionwesterns